C000058772

THE BEAUX-STRATAGEM

CONTENTS

PREFACE

The Author. 'It is surprising,' says Mr. Percy Fitzgerald, 'how much English Comedy owes to Irishmen.' Nearly fifty years ago Calcraft enumerated eighty-seven Irish dramatists in a by no means exhaustive list, including Congreve, Southerne, Steele, Kelly, Macklin, and Farquhar—the really Irish representative amongst the dramatists of the Restoration, the true prototype of Goldsmith and Sheridan. Thoroughly Irish by birth and education, Captain George Farquhar (1677-1707) had delighted the town with a succession of bright, rattling comedies—Love and a Bottle (1698), The Constant Couple (1699), Sir Harry Wildair (1701), The Inconstant (1702), The Twin Rivals (1702), The Recruiting Officer (1706). In an unlucky moment, when hard pressed by his debts, he sold out of the army on the strength of a promise by the Duke of Ormond to gain him some preferment, which never came. In his misery and poverty, with a wife and two helpless girls to support, Farquhar was not forsaken by his one true friend, Robert Wilks. Seeking out the dramatist in his wretched garret in St Martin's Lane, the actor advised him no longer to trust to great men's promises, but to look only to his pen for support, and urged him to write another play. 'Write!' said Farquhar, starting from his chair; 'is it possible that a man can write with common-sense who is heartless and has not a shilling in his pockets?' 'Come, come, George,' said Wilks, 'banish melancholy, draw up your drama, and bring your sketch with you to-morrow, for I expect you to dine with me. But as an empty purse may cramp your genius, I desire you to accept my mite; here is twenty guineas.' Farquhar set to work, and brought the plot of his play to Wilks the next day; the later approved the design, and urged him to proceed without delay. Mostly written in bed, the whole was begun, finished, and acted within six weeks. The author designed to dedicate it to Lord Cadogan, but his lordship, for reasons unknown, declined the honour; he gave the dramatist a handsome present, however. Thus was *The Beaux-Stratagem* written. Farquhar is said to have felt the approaches of death ere he finished the second act. On the night of the first performance Wilks came to tell him of his great success, but mentioned that Mrs. Oldfield wished that he could have thought of some more legitimate divorce in order to secure the honour of Mrs. Sullen. 'Oh,' said Farquhar, 'I will, if she pleases, solve that immediately, by getting a real divorce; marrying her myself, and giving her my bond that she shall be a widow in less than a fortnight.' Subsequent events practically fulfilled this prediction, for Farquhar died during the run of the play: on the day of his extra benefit, Tuesday, 29th April 1707, the plaudits of the audience resounding in his ears, the destitute, broken-hearted dramatist passed to that bourne where stratagems avail not any longer.

Criticism of The Beaux-Stratagem. Each play that Farquhar produced was an improvement on its predecessors, and all critics have been unanimous in pronouncing *The Beaux-Stratagem* his best, both in the study and on the stage, of which it retained possession much the longest. Except *The Recruiting Officer* and *The Inconstant*, revived at Covent Garden in 1825, and also by Daly in America in 1885, none of Farquhar's other plays has been put on the stage for upwards of a century. Hallam says: 'Never has Congreve equalled *The Beaux-Stratagem* in vivacity, in originality of contrivance, or in clear and rapid development of intrigue'; and Hazlitt considers it 'sprightly lively, bustling, and full of point and interest: the assumed disguise of Archer and Aimwell is a perpetual amusement to the mind.' The action—which commences, remarkably briskly, in the evening and ends about midnight the next day—never flags for an instant. The well-contrived plot is original and simple (all Farquhar's plots are excellent), giving rise to a rapid succession of amusing and sensational incidents; though by no means extravagant or improbable, save possibly the mutual separation of Squire Sullen and his wife in the last scene—the weak point of the whole. Farquhar was a master in stage-effect. Aimwell's stratagem of passing himself off as the wealthy nobleman, his brother (a device previously adopted by Vanbrugh in *The Relapse* and subsequently by Sheridan in his *Trip to Scarborough*), may perhaps be a covert allusion to the romantic story of the dramatist's own deception by the penniless lady who gave herself out to be possessed of a large fortune, and who thus induced him to marry her.

The style adopted is highly dramatic, the dialogue being natural and flowing; trenchant and sprightly, but not too witty for a truthful reflex of actual conversation. The humour is genial and unforced; there is no smell of the lamp about it, no premeditated effort at dragging in jests, as in Congreve. As typical examples of Farquhar's *vis comica* I Would cite the description of Squire Sullen's home-coming, and his 'pot of ale' speech, Aimwell's speech respecting conduct at church, the scene between Cherry and Archer about the £2000, and the final separation scene—which affords a curious view of the marriage tie and on which Leigh Hunt has founded an argument for divorce. This play contains several examples of Farquhar's curious habit of breaking out into a kind of broken blank verse occasionally for a few lines in the more serious passages. Partaking as it does of the elements of both comedy and force, it is the prototype of Goldsmith's *She Stoops to Conquer*, which it resembles in many respects. It will be remembered that Miss Hardcastle compares herself to Cherry (Act III.), and young Marlow and Hastings much resemble Archer and Aimwell. Goldsmith was a great admirer of the works of his fellow-countryman, especially *The Beaux-Stratagem*, and refers to them several times (Citizen of the World, letter 93; History of England, letter 16; Vicar of Wakefield, ch. 18), and in the Literary Magazine for 1758 he drew up a curious poetical scale in which he classes the Restoration dramatists thus:—Congreve—Genius 15, Judgment 16, Learning 14, Versification 14; Vanbrugh—14, 15,14,10; Farquhar—15, 15, 10, io. Unlike Goldsmith, unhappily, Farquhar's moral tone is not high; sensuality is confounded with love, ribaldry mistaken for wit The best that can be said of him that he contrasts favourably with his contemporary dramatists; Virtue is not *always* uninteresting in his pages. He is free from their heartlessness, malignity, and cruelty. The plot of *The Beaux-Stratagem* is comparatively inoffensive, and the moral of the whole is healthy. Although a wit rather than a thinker, Farquhar in this play shows himself capable of serious feelings. It is remarkable how much Farquhar repeats himself. Hardly an allusion or idea occurs in this play that is not to be found elsewhere in his works. In the Notes I have pointed out many of these coincidences.

The Characters. This play has added several distinct original personages to our stock of comedy characters, and it affords an excellent and lifelike picture of a peculiar and perishing phase of the manners of the time, especially those obtaining in the country house, and the village inn frequented by highwaymen. The sly, rascally landlord, Boniface (who has given his name to the class), is said to have been drawn from life, and his portrait, we are told, was still to be seen at Lichfield in 1775. The inimitable 'brother Scrub,' that 'indispensable appendage to a country gentleman's kitchen' (Hazlitt), with his ignorance and shrewd eye to the main chance, is likewise said to have been a well-known personage who survived till 1759, one Thomas Bond, servant to Sir Theophilus Biddulph; others say he died at Salisbury in 1744. Although Farquhar, like Goldsmith, undoubtedly drew his incidents and personages from his own daily associations, there is probably no more truth in these surmises than in the assertion (repeatedly made, though denied in his preface to *The Inconstant*) that Farquhar depicts himself in his young heroes, his rollicking 'men about town,' Roebuck, Mirabel, Wildair, Plume, Archer. Archer (copied by Hoadley in his character of Ranger in *The Suspicious Husband*) is a decided improvement on his predecessors, and is the best of all Farquhar's creations; he is assuredly the most brilliant footman that ever was, eminently sociable and, with all his easy, rattling volubility, never forgetful of his self-respect and never indifferent to the wishes or welfare of others. As Hunt has pointed out, the characters of Archer and

Aimwell improve as the play progresses; they set out as mere intriguers, but prove in the end true gentlemen. They are sad rogues, no doubt, but they have no bitter cynicism, no meanness; Aimwell refuses to marry Dorinda under any deception. They thoroughly good fellows at bottom, manly, accomplished his spirited, eloquent, generous—the forerunners of Charles Surfor. Marriage retrieves them and turns them into respectable and adoring husbands. Though rattle-brained, much given to gallantry, and somewhat lax in morality, they are not knaves or monsters; they do not inspire disgust. Even the lumpish blockhead, Squire Sullen—according to Macaulay a type of the main strength of the Tory party for half a century after the Revolution—contrasts favourably with his prototype Sir John Brute in Vanbrugh's *Provoked Wife*, He is a sodden sot, who always goes to bed drunk, but he is not a demon; he does not beat his wife in public; he observes common decency somewhat. His wife is a witty, attractive, warm-hearted woman, whose faults are transparent; the chief one being that she has made the fatal mistake of marrying for fortune and position instead of for love. There is something pathetic in her position which claims our sympathy. She is well contrasted with her sister-in-law, the sincere, though somewhat weakly drawn, Dorinda; whilst their mother-in-law, Lady Bountiful, famed for her charity, is an amusing and gracious figure, which has often been copied. Cherry, with her honest heart and her quickness of perception, is also a distinct creation. Strange to say, the only badly drawn character is Foigard, the unscrupulous Irish Jesuit priest. Farquhar is fond of introducing an Irishman into each of his plays, but I cannot say that I think he is generally successful; certainly not in this instance. They are mostly broad caricatures, and speak an outlandish jargon, more like Welsh than Irish, supposed to be the Ulster dialect: anything more unlike it would be difficult to conceive. The early conventional stage Irishman, tracing him from Captain. Macmorris in Henry V.,through Ben Jonson's *Irish Masque* and *New Inn*, Dekker's Bryan, Ford's Mayor of Cork, Shadwell's O'Divelly (probably Farquhar's model for Foigard), is truly a wondrous savage, chiefly distinguished by his use of the expletives 'Dear Joy!' and 'By Creesh!' This character naturally rendered the play somewhat unpopular in Ireland, and its repulsiveness is unrelieved (as it is in the case of Teague in *The Twin Rivals*) by a single touch of humour or native comicality. It is an outrage.

The First Performance. The Beaux-Stratagem was first performed on Saturday, 8th March 1707, at the Theatre Royal (or, as it was sometimes called, the Queen's Theatre), situated in the Haymarket, on the site afterwards occupied by Her Majesty's Theatre. It ran for ten nights only, owing to benefits. The cast on that occasion was a strong one. Robert Wilks (a brother-Irishman), who performed Archer, was the foremost actor of the day. He was Farquhar's lifelong friend, and appeared in all his plays, except *Love and a Bottle* which was produced in London during Wilks's absence in Dublin. This actor's most famous part was 'Sir Harry Wildair' (*The Constant Couple*), which our author drew on purpose for him, and which ran for fifty-two nights on its first appearance. Farquhar himself said that when the stage had the misfortune to lose Wilks, 'Sir Harry Wildair' might go to the Jubilee! Peg Woffington is said to have been his only rival in this part. Sullen was the last original character undertaken by Verbruggen, a leading actor of the time. It was from Verbruggen's wife (probably the 'Mrs. V—' of Farquhar's letters) that the famous Mrs. Oldfield received her earliest instructions in acting. The last-named lady was the original Mrs. Sullen. Her connection with Farquhar is very interesting and romantic. She resided with her aunt, Mrs. Voss, who kept the Mitre Tavern in St, James's Market (between Jeryrm Street, Regent Street, and the Haymarket). One day, when she was aged sixteen, Farquhar, a smart young captain of twenty-two, happened to be dining there, and he overheard her reading Beaumont and Fletcher's *Scornful Lady* aloud behind the bar. When Farquhar, much struck by her musical delivery and expression, pressed her to resume her reading, the tall and graceful girl consented with hesitation and bashfulness; although she afterwards confessed, 'I longed to be at it, and only needed a decent entreaty.' The dramatist quickly acquainted Sir John Vanbrugh with the jewel he had thus accidentally found, and she obtained through him an engagement at the Theatre Royal as 'Candiope' in Dryden's *Secret Love*. She soon became the fine lady of the stage, and was the original representative of no less than sixty-five characters. Pope disliked and satirised her severely; on the other hand, Cibber worshipped her. According to some, Farquhar fell violently in love with her, and she is the 'Penelope' of his letters; but although she often spoke of the happy hours she spent in his company, there appears to be no foundation for this surmise. Bowen, a low comedian of considerable talent, afterwards accidentally killed by Quin the actor, was Foigard; and Scrub—originally written for Colley Cibber, who, however, preferred Gibbet—was represented by Norris, a capital comic actor, universally known as 'Jubilee Dicky' on account of his representation of 'Dicky' in *The Constant Couple*. He had an odd, formal little figure, and a high squeaking voice; if he came into a coffee-house and merely called 'Waiter!' everybody present felt inclined to laugh. He had previously appeared in Farquhar's four principal plays, as also had Mills, who did Aimwell. Cibber tells us that the play was better received at Drury Lane than at the Haymarket, as, owing to the larger size of the latter house, it was difficult to hear.

Later Stage History. Originally brought out under the title *The Stratagem* only, which it retained in the playbills till 1787 (though printed with 'Beaux'), this play continued to be very popular with the stage down to the dawn of the present century; and many great actors and actresses appeared from time to time in its characters; In 1721 Quin acted in Lincoln's Inn Fields as Squire Sullen. The part of Mrs. Sullen has been undertaken by Mrs. Pritchard (1740 and 1761), Peg Woffington (1742, along with Garrick as Archer for the first time, and Macklin as Scrub), Mrs. Abington (1774, 1785, 1798), Mrs. Barry (1778), Miss Farren (1779), Mrs. Jordan (1802), Mrs. C. Kemble (1810), Mrs. Davison (1818), and Miss Chester (1823, for Dibdin's benefit, with Liston as Scrub). Garrick's repeated performances of Archer, in light blue and silver livery, were supremely good, more particularly in the scenes with Cherry, the picture scene with Mrs. Sullen, and when he delivers Lady Howd'ye's message. He generally acted with Weston, an inimitable Scrub; but at O'Brien's benefit at Drury Lane, 10th April 1761, Garrick himself played Scrub to O'Brien's Archer. On one occasion Garrick had refused Weston a loan of money, and Weston not appearing at the greenroom, Garrick came forward before the curtain and announced that he would himself play Scrub, as Weston was ill. Weston, who was in the gallery with a sham bailiff, shouted out, 'I am here, but the bailiff won't let me come '; whereupon the audience insisted on Garrick's paying the loan and relieving the debtor so as to enable him to play Scrub! Other famous Scrubs were Shutes (1774), Quick (1778, 1785, 1798), Bannister, junior (1802, will C. Kemble as Aimwell), Dowton (1802), Liston (1810), Johnstone (1821), and Keeley (1828, with C. Kemble as Arches and Miss Foote as Cherry; it ran for twelve nights at Covenl Garden). Goldsmith is said to have expressed a desire to art this part. On the occasion of Mrs. Abington's benefit (Covenl Garden, November 19, 1785), she took the part of Scrub for that night only, for a wager, it is said. Ladies were desired to send their servants to retain seats by four o'clock, and the pit and boxes were laid together. She disgraced herself, acting the part with her hair dressed for 'Lady Racket' in the afterpiece (*Three Hours After Marriage*). In April 1823 another female impersonator of this part appeared—not very successfully—in Miss Clara Fisher, with Farren as Archer. This was in Dublin (Hawkins' Street), where the play was frequently performed about 1821-1823. It was also the piece chosen for the re-opening of Smock Alley Theatre, Dublin, in 1759, when Mrs. Abington made her first appearance on the Irish stage as Mrs. Sullen.

Miss Pope (1774), Mrs. Martyn (1785, 1798), and Mrs. Gibbs (1819) were the principal exponents of Cherry. In 1819 Emery did Gibbet.

About 1810 the play was performed at the Royal Circus under Elliston as a *ballet d'action*, in order to evade the Patent Act. Otherwise, neither this play nor any other of Farquhar's seems ever to have been 'adapted' for the modern stage. In the present half-century *The Beaux-Stratagem* has been but seldom performed. It was acted in London in 1856. In February 1878 Mr.

Phelps gave it extremely well in the Annexe Theatre at the Westminster Aquarium. Lastly, William Farren, as Archer, revived it at the Imperial Theatre, on Monday, 22nd September 1879, with great success, a new Prologue (spoken by Mrs. Stirling) being written for the occasion. There were several matinees given in succession. The cast included Mr. Kyrle Bellew as Gibbet; Mr. Lionel Brough as Scrub; Miss Marie Litton as Mrs. Sullen; Mrs. Stirling—one of her last appearances—as Lady Bountiful; Dorinda, Miss Meyrick; Cherry, Miss Carlotta Addison; Gipsy, Miss Passinger; Aimwell, Mr. Edgar; Sir Charles Freeman, Mr. Denny; Sullen, Mr. Ryder; Foigard, Mr. Bannister; Boniface, Mr. Everill; Hounslow, Mr. Bunch; Bagshot, Mr. Leitch. The Epilogue for this occasion was written by Mr. Clement Scott. I know not if the play has been acted since that date.

Bibliography. The first edition was published in a small quarto (78 pages) by Bernard Lintott, 'at the Cross-Keys next Nando's Coffeehouse in Fleet Street' between the two Temple gates. The British Museum Catalogue dates it 1707 (the copy in my possession, however, bears no date), but it is supposed not to have been published till 1710, three years after Farquhar's decease; whence some have erroneously dated his death in that year. Lintott, on January 27, 1707, had paid the dramatist £30. in advance for this play, double what he usually gave for a play. The same publisher issued the first complete edition of Farquhar's plays in an octavo volume, dedicated to John Eyre, with a quaint illustration prefixed to each play (we reproduce that prefixed to *The Beaux-Stratagem*), introducing all the characters of the play, and a frontispiece representing Farquhar being presented to Apollo by Ben Jonson. The general title-page is undated, but the title-pages of the various plays bear the date 1711, and all bear Lintott's name (sometimes alone, sometimes with others) save *Sir Harry Wildair*, which is said to be printed by James Knapton. Some say this volume did not appear till 1714. In 1760 Rivington published an edition of Farquhar which appears to be slightly 'bowdlerised.' At least two complete editions of his works were published in Dublin; one, described as the seventh, in two volumes small octavo, by Risk and Smith, in 1743 (including a memoir, and *Love and Business*), in which the title-pages of the various plays bear different dates, ranging from 1727 to 1741, *The Beaux-Stratagem* being described as the twelfth edition, and dated 1739; the other, charmingly printed by Ewing in three 16mo volumes, dated 1775, with a vignette portrait and other illustrations, and containing a life by Thomas Wilkes. An Edinburgh edition of The *Beaux-Stratagem*, with life, appeared in 1768, and an edition in German in 1782 by J. Leonhardi, under the title *Die Stutzerlist*. Separate editions of the play also appeared in 1748, 1778, and 1824 (New York), and it is included in all the various collections of English plays, such as Bell's, Oxberry's, Inchbald's, Dibdin's, Cumberland's, etc., and in the collected editions of Farquhar's works dated 1718, 1728, 1736, 1742, 1760, and 1772. The principal modern editions of Farquhar are Leigh Hunt's (along with Wycherley, Vanbrugh, and Congreve), and Ewald's (1892), in two volumes large octavo.

ADVERTISEMENT

The reader may find some faults in this play, which my illness prevented the amending of; but there is great amends made in the representation, which cannot be matched, no more than the friendly and indefatigable care of Mr. Wilks, to whom I chiefly owe the success of the play.

GEORGE FARQUHAR.

DRAMATIS PERSONAE

With names of the original actors and actresses.

DRAMATIS PERSONÆ

With names of the original actors and actresses.

MEN

Thomas Aimwell, Francis Archer,	Two gentlemen of broken fortunes, the first as master, and the second as servant,	Mr. Mills. Mr. Wilks.
Count Bellair,	A French Officer, prisoner at Lichfield,	Mr. Boman.
Squire Sullen,	A Country Blockhead, brutal to his Wife,	Mr. Verbrug
Sir Charles Freeman,	A Gentleman from London, brother to Mrs. Sullen,	Mr. Keen.
Foigard,	A Priest, Chaplain to the French Officers,	Mr Bowen.
Gibbet,	A Highwayman,	Mr. Cibber.
Hounslow, Bagshot,	His Companions.	
Boniface,	Landlord of the Inn,	Mr. Bullock
Scrub,	Servant to Squire Sullen,	Mr. Norris.

WOMEN

Lady Bountiful,	An old, civil, Country Gentlewoman, that cures all her neighbours of all distempers, and foolishly fond of her son, Squire Sullen,	Mrs. Powell
Mrs. Sullen,	Her Daughter-in-law, wife to Squire Sullen,	Mrs. Oldfiel
Dorinda,	Lady Bountiful's Daughter,	Mrs. Bradsh
Gipsy,	Maid to the Ladies,	Mrs. Mills
Cherry,	The Landlord's Daughter in the Inn,	Mrs. Bicknel

Tapster, Coach-passengers, Countryman, Countrywoman, and Servants.

SCENE—Lichfield.

PROLOGUE

Spoken by Mr. Wilks.

WHEN strife disturbs, or sloth corrupts an age, Keen satire is the business of the stage. When the *Plain-Dealer* writ, he lash'd those crimes, Which then infested most—the modish times: But now, when faction sleeps, and sloth is fled, And all our youth in active fields are bred; When through Great Britain's fair extensive round, The trumps of fame, the notes of UNION sound; When Anna's sceptre points the laws their course, And her example gives her precepts force: There scarce is room for satire; all our lays Must be, or songs of triumph, or of praise. But as in grounds best cultivated, tares And poppies rise among the golden ears; Our product so, fit for the field or school, Must mix with nature's favourite plant—a fool: A weed that has to twenty summers ran, Shoots up in stalk, and vegetates to man. Simpling our author goes from field to field, And culls such fools as many diversion yield And, thanks to Nature, there's no want of those, For rain or shine, the thriving coxcomb grows. Follies to-night we show ne'er lash'd before, Yet such as nature shows you every hour; Nor can the pictures give a just offence, For fools are made for jests to men of sense.

ACT I., SCENE I.

A Room in Bonifaces Inn. Enter Boniface running.

Bon. Chamberlain! maid! Cherry! daughter Cherry! all asleep? all dead?

Enter Cherry running.

Cher. Here, here! why d'ye bawl so, father? d'ye think we have no ears?

Bon. You deserve to have none, you young minx! The company of the Warrington coach has stood in the hall this hour, and nobody to show them to their chambers.

Cher. And let 'em wait farther; there's neither red-coat in the coach, nor footman behind it.

Bon. But they threaten to go to another inn to-night.

Cher. That they dare not, for fear the coachman should overturn them to-morrow.—Coming! coming!—Here's the London coach arrived.

Enter several people with trunks, bandboxes, and other luggage, and cross the stage.

Bon. Welcome, ladies!

Cher. Very welcome, gentlemen!—Chamberlain, show the *Lion and the Rose.* [*Exit with the company.*

Enter Aimwell in a riding-habit, and Archer as footman, c arrying a portmantle.

25

Bon. This way, this way, gentlemen!

Aim. [*To Archer.*] Set down the things; go to the stable, and see my horses well rubbed.

Arch. I shall, sir. [*Exit.*

Aim. You're my landlord, I suppose?

Bon. Yes, sir, I 'm old Will Boniface, pretty well known upon this road, as the saying is.

Aim. O Mr. Boniface, your servant!

Bon. O sir!—What will your honour please to drink, as the saying is?

Aim. I have heard your town of Lichfield much famed for ale; I think I 'll taste that.

Bon. Sir, I have now in my cellar ten tun of the best ale in Staffordshire; 'tis smooth as oil, sweet as milk, clear as amber, and strong as brandy; and will be just fourteen year old the fifth day of next March, old style.

Aim. You're very exact, I find, in the age of your ale.

Bon. As punctual, sir, as I am in the age of my children. I'll show you such ale!—Here, tapster [*Enter Tapster*] broach number 1706, as the saying is.—Sir, you shall taste my *Anno Domini.*—I have lived in Lichfield, man and boy, above eight-and-fifty years, and, I believe, have not consumed eight-and-fifty ounces of meat.

Aim. At a meal, you mean, if one may guess your sense by your bulk.

Bon. Not in my life, sir: I have fed purely upon ale; I have eat my ale, drank my ale, and I always sleep upon ale.

Enter Tapster with a bottle and glass, and exit.

Now, sir, you shall see!—[*Fitting out a glass.*] Your worship's health.—[*Drinks.*] Ha! delicious, delicious! fancy it burgundy, only fancy it, and 'tis worth ten shillings a quart.

Aim. [Drinks,] 'Tis confounded strong!

Bon. Strong! it must be so, or how should we be strong that drink it?

Aim. And have you lived so long upon this ale, landlord?

Bon. Eight-and-fifty years, upon my credit, sir—but it killed my wife, poor woman, as the saying is.

Aim. How came that to pass?

Bon. I don't know how, sir; she would not let the ale take its natural course, sir; she was for qualifying it every now and then with a dram, as the saying is; and an honest gentleman that came this way from Ireland, made her a present of a dozen bottles of usquebaugh—but the poor woman was never well after: but, howe'er, I was obliged to the gentleman, you know.

Aim. Why, was it the usquebaugh that killed her?

Bon. My Lady Bountiful said so. She, good lady, did what could be done; she cured her of three tympanies, but the fourth carried her off. But she's happy, and I 'm contented, as the saying is.

Aim. Who 's that Lady Bountiful you mentioned?

Bon. 'Ods my life, sir, we'll drink her health.—[Drinks.] My Lady Bountiful is one of the best of women. Her last husband, Sir Charles Bountiful, left her worth a thousand pound, a year; and, I believe, she lays out one-half on't in charitable uses for the good of her neighbours. She cures rheumatisms, ruptures, and broken shins in men; green-sickness, obstructions, and fits of the mother, in women; the king's evil, chincough, and chilblains, in children: in short, she has cured more people in and about Lichfield within ten years than the doctors have killed in twenty; and that's a bold word.

Aim. Has the lady been any other way useful in her generation?

Bon. Yes, sir; she has a daughter by Sir Charles, the finest woman in all our country, and the greatest *fortune*. She has a son too, by her first husband, Squire Sullen, who married a fine lady from London t' other day; if you please, sir, we 'll drink his health.

Aim. What sort of a man is he?

Bon. Why, sir, the man 's well enough; says little, thinks less, and does—nothing at all, faith. But he's a man of a great estate, and values nobody.

Aim. A sportsman, I suppose?

Bon. Yes, sir, he's a man of pleasure; he plays at whisk and smokes his pipe eight-and-forty hours together sometimes.

Aim. And married, you say?

Bon. Ay, and to a curious woman, sir. But he's a—he wants it here, sir. [*Pointing to his forehead.*

Aim. He has it there, you mean?

Bon. That's none of my business; he's my landlord, and so a man, you know, would not—But—ecod, he's no better than—Sir, my humble service to you.—[*Drinks.*] Though I value not a farthing what he can do to me; I pay him his rent at quarter-day; I have a good running-trade; I have but one daughter, and I can give her—but no matter for that.

Aim. You're very happy, Mr. Boniface. Pray, what other company have you in town?

Bon. A power of fine ladies; and then we have the French officers.

Aim. Oh, that's right, you have a good many of those gentlemen: pray, how do you like their company?

Bon. So well, as the saying is, that I could wish we had as many more of 'em; they're full of money, and pay double for everything they have. They know, sir, that we paid good round taxes for the taking of 'em, and so they are willing to reimburse us a little. One of 'em lodges in my house.

Re-enter Archer.

Arch. Landlord, there are some French gentlemen below that ask for you.

Bon. I'll wait on 'em.—[*Aside to Archer.*] Does your master stay long in town, as the saying is?

Arch. I can't tell, as the saying is.

Bon. Come from London?

Arch. No.

Bon. Going to London, mayhap?

Arch. No.

Bon. [*Aside.*] An odd fellow this.—[*To Aimwell.*] I beg your worship's pardon, I 'll wait on you in half a minute. [*Exit.*

Aim. The coast's clear, I see.—Now, my dear Archer, welcome to Lichfield!

Arch. I thank thee, my dear brother in iniquity.

Aim. Iniquity! prithee, leave canting; you need not change your style with your dress.

Arch. Don't mistake me, Aimwell, for 'tis still my maxim, that there is no scandal like rags, nor any crime so shameful as poverty.

Aim. The world confesses it every day in its practice though men won't own it for their opinion. Who did that worthy lord my brother, single out of the side-box to sup with him t' other night?

Arch. Jack Handicraft, a handsome, well-dressed, mannerly, sharping rogue, who keeps the best company in town.

Aim. Right!' And, pray, who married my lady Manslaughter t'other day, the great fortune?

Arch. Why, Nick Marrabone, a professed pickpocket, and a good bowler; but he makes a handsome figure, and rides in his coach, that he formerly used to ride behind.

Aim. But did you observe poor Jack Generous in the Park last week.

Arch. Yes, with his autumnal periwig, shading his melancholy face, his coat older than anything but its fashion, with one hand idle in his pocket, and with the other picking his useless teeth; and, though the Mall was crowded with company, yet was poor Jack as single and solitary as a lion in a desert.

Aim. And as much avoided for no crime upon earth but the want of money.

Arch. And that's enough. Men must not be poor; idleness is the root of all evil; the world's wide enough, let 'em bustle. Fortune has taken the weak under her protection, but men of sense are left to their industry.

Aim. Upon which topic we proceed, and, I think, luckily hitherto. Would not any man swear now, that I am a man of quality, and you my servant, when if our intrinsic value were known—

Arch. Come, come, we are the men of intrinsic value who can strike our fortunes out of ourselves, whose worth is independent of accidents in life, or revolutions in government: we have heads to get money and hearts to spend it.

Aim. As to pur hearts, I grant ye, they are as willing tits as any within twenty degrees: but I can have no great opinion of our heads from the service they have done us hitherto, unless it be that they have brought us from London hither to Lichfield, made me a lord and you my servant.

Arch. That 's more than you could expect already. But what money have we left?

Aim. But two hundred pound.

Arch. And our horses, clothes, rings, etc.—Why, we have very good fortunes now for moderate people; and, let me tell you, that this two hundred pound, with the experience that we are now masters of, is a better estate than the ten we have spent—Our friends, indeed, began to suspect that our pockets were low, but we came off with flying colours, showed no signs of want either in word or deed.

Aim. Ay, and our going to Brussels was a good pretence enough for our sudden disappearing; and, I warrant you, our friends imagine that we are gone a-volunteering.

Arch. Why, faith, if this prospect fails, it must e'en come to that I am for venturing one of the hundreds, if you will, upon this knight-errantry; but, in case it should fail, we 'll reserve t' other to carry us to some counterscarp, where we may die, as we lived, in a blaze.

Aim. With all my heart; and we have lived justly, Archer: we can't say that we have spent our fortunes, but that we have enjoyed 'em.

Arch. Right! so much pleasure for so much money. We have had our pennyworths; and, had I millions, I would go to the same market again.—O London! London!—Well, we have had our share, and let us be thankful: past pleasures, for aught I know, are best, such as we are sure of; those to come may disappoint us.

Aim. It has often grieved the heart of me to see how some inhuman wretches murder their kind fortunes; those that, by sacrificing all to one appetite, shall starve all the rest. You shall have some that live only in their palates, and in their sense of tasting shall drown the other four: others are only epicures in appearances, such who shall starve their nights to make a figure a days, and famish their own to feed the eyes of others: a contrary sort confine their pleasures to the dark, and contract their specious acres to the circuit of a muff-string.

Arch. Right! But they find the Indies in that spot where they consume 'em, and I think your kind keepers have much the best on't: for they indulge the most senses by one expense, there's the seeing, hearing, and feeling, amply gratified; and, some philosophers will tell you, that from such a commerce there arises a sixth sense, that gives infinitely more pleasure than the other five put together,

Aim. And to pass to the other extremity, of all keepers I think those the worst that keep their money.

Arch. Those are the most miserable wights in being, they destroy the rights of nature, and disappoint the blessings of Providence. Give me a man that keeps his five senses keen and bright as his sword, that has 'em always drawn out in their just order and strength, with his reason as commander at the head of 'em, that detaches 'em by turns upon whatever party of pleasure agreeably offers, and commands 'em to retreat upon the least appearance of disadvantage or danger! For my part, I can stick to my bottle while my wine, my company, and my reason, hold good; I can be charmed with Sappho's singing without falling in love with her face: I love hunting, but would not, like Actæon, be eaten up by my own dogs; I love a fine house, but let another keep it; and just so I love a fine woman.

Aim. In that last particular you have the better of me.

Arch. Ay, you're such an amorous puppy, that I'm afraid you 'll spoil our sport; you can't counterfeit the passion without feeling it.

Aim. Though the whining part be out of doors in town, 'tis still in force with the country ladies: and let me tell you, Frank, the fool in that passion shall-outdo the knave at any time.

Arch. Well, I won't dispute it now; you command for the day, and so I submit: at Nottingham, you know, I am to be master.

Aim. And at Lincoln, I again.

Arch. Then, at Norwich I mount, which, I think, shall be our last stage; for, if we fail there, we'll embark for Holland, bid adieu to Venus, and welcome Mars.

Aim. A match!—Mum!

Re-enter Boniface.

Bon. What will your worship please to have for supper?

Aim. What have you got?

Bon. Sir, we have a delicate piece of beef in the pot, and a pig at the fire.

Aim. Good supper-meat, I must confess. I can't eat beef, landlord.

Arch. And I hate pig.

Aim. Hold your prating, sirrah! do you know who you are?

Bon. Please to bespeak something else; I have everything in the house.

Aim. Have you any veal?

Bon. Veal! sir, we had a delicate loin of veal on Wednesday last.

Aim. Have you got any fish or wildfowl?

Bon. As for fish, truly, sir, we are an inland town, and indifferently provided with fish, that 's the truth on't; and then for wildfowl—we have a delicate couple of rabbits.

Aim. Get me the rabbits fricasseed.

Bon. Fricasseed! Lard, sir, they 'll eat much better smothered with onions.

Arch. Psha! Damn your onions!

Aim. Again, sirrah!—Well, landlord, what you please. But hold, I have a small charge of money, and your house is so full of strangers that I believe it may be safer in your custody than mine; for when this fellow of mine gets drunk he tends to nothing.—Here, sirrah, reach me the strong-box.

Arch. Yes, sir.—[*Aside.*] This will give us a reputation.

[*Brings Aimwell the box.*

Aim. Here, landlord; the locks are sealed down both for your security and mine; it holds somewhat above two hundred pound: if you doubt it I'll count it to you after supper; but be sure you lay it where I may have it at a minute's warning; for my affairs are a little dubious at present; perhaps I may be gone in half an hour, perhaps I may be your guest till the best part of that be spent; and pray order your ostler to keep my horses always saddled. But one thing above the rest I must beg, that you would let this fellow have none of your *Anno Domini*, as you call it; for he's the most insufferable sot—Here, sirrah, light me to my chamber.

[*Exit, lighted by Archer.*

Bon. Cherry! daughter Cherry!

Re-enter Cherry.

33

Cher. D'ye call, father?

Bon. Ay, child, you must lay by this box for the gentleman: 'tis full of money.

Cher. Money! all that money! why, sure, father, the gentleman comes to be chosen parliament-man. Who is he?

Bon. I don't know what to make of him; he talks of keeping his horses ready saddled, and of going perhaps at a minute's warning, or of staying perhaps till the best part of this be spent.

Cher. Ay, ten to one, father, he's a highwayman.

Bon. A highwayman! upon my life, girl, you have hit it, and this box is some new-purchased booty. Now, could we find him out, the money were ours.

Cher. He don't belong to our gang.

Bon. What horses have they?

Cher. The master rides upon a black.

Bon. A black! ten to one the man upon the black mare; and since he don't belong to our fraternity, we may betray him with a safe conscience: I don't think it lawful to harbour any rogues but my own. Look'ee, child, as the saying is, we must go cunningly to work, proofs we must have; the gentleman's servant loves drink, I'll ply him that way, and ten to one loves a wench: you must work him t' other way.

Cher. Father, would you have me give my secret for his?

Bon. Consider, child, there's two hundred pound to boot.—[*Ringing without.*] Coming! coming!—Child, mind your business. [*Exit.*

Cher. What a rogue is my father! My father! I deny it. My mother was a good, generous, free-hearted woman, and I can't tell how far her good nature might have extended for the good of her children. This landlord of mine, for I think I can call him no more, would betray his guest, and debauch his daughter into the bargain—by a footman too!

Re-enter Archer.

Arch. What footman, pray, mistress, is so happy as to be the subject of your contemplation?

Cher. Whoever he is, friend, he'll be but little the better for't.

Arch. I hope so, for, I 'm sure, you did not think of me.

Cher. Suppose I had?

Arch. Why, then, you 're but even with me; for the minute I came in, I was a-considering in what manner I should make love to you.

Cher. Love to me, friend!

Arch. Yes, child.

Cher. Child! manners!—If you kept a little more distance, friend, it would become you much better.

Arch. Distance! good-night, sauce-box. [*Going.*

Cher. [*Aside.*] A pretty fellow! I like his pride.—[*Aloud.*] Sir, pray, sir, you see, sir [*Archer returns*] I have the credit to be entrusted with your master's fortune here, which sets me a degree above his footman; I hope, sir, you an't affronted?

Arch. Let me look you full in the face, and I 'll tell you whether you can affront me or no. 'Sdeath, child, you have a pair of delicate eyes, and you don't know what to do with 'em!

Cher. Why, sir, don't I see everybody?

Arch. Ay, but if some women had 'em, they would kill everybody. Prithee, instruct me, I would fain make love to you, but I don't know what to say.

Cher. Why, did you never make love to anybody before?

Arch. Never to a person of your figure I can assure you, madam: my addresses have been always confined to people within my own sphere, I never aspired so high before. [*Sings.*

But you look so bright,
And are dress'd so tight,
That a man would swear you 're right,
As arm was e'er laid over.

Such an air
You freely wear
To ensnare,
As makes each guest a lover!

Since then, my dear, I 'm your guest,
Prithee give me of the best
Of what is ready drest:
Since then, my dear, etc.

Cher. [*Aside.*] What can I think of this man?—[*Aloud.*] Will you give me that song, sir?

Arch. Ay, my dear, take it while 'tis warm.—[*Kisses her.*] Death and fire! her lips are honeycombs.

Cher. And I wish there had been bees too, to have stung you for your impudence.

Arch. There 's a swarm of Cupids, my little Venus, that has done the business much better.

Cher. [*Aside.*] This fellow is misbegotten as well as I.—[Aloud.] What's your name, sir?

Arch. [*Aside.*] Name! egad, I have forgot it.—[*Aloud.*] Oh! Martin.

Cher. Where were you born?

Arch. In St Martin's parish.

Cher. What was your father?

Arch. St. Martin's parish.

Cher. Then, friend, good-night

Arch. I hope not.

Cher. You may depend upon't

Arch. Upon what?

Cher. That you're very impudent.

Arch. That you 're very handsome.

Cher. That you're a footman.

Arch. That you're an angel.

Cher. I shall be rude.

Arch. So shall I.

Cher. Let go my hand.

Arch. Give me a kiss. [*Kisses her.*

[*Call without.*] Cherry! Cherry!

Cher. I'm—my father calls; you plaguy devil, how durst you stop my breath so? Offer to follow me one step, if you dare. [*Exit.*

Arch. A fair challenge, by this light! this is a pretty fair opening of an adventure; but we are knight-errants, and so Fortune be our guide. [*Exit.*

ACT II., SCENE I.

A Gallery in Lady Bountiful's House. Enter Mrs. Sullen and Dorinda, meeting.

Dor. Morrow, my dear sister; are you for church this morning?

Mrs. Sul. Anywhere to pray; for Heaven alone can help me. But I think, Dorinda, there's no form of prayer in the liturgy against bad husbands:

Dor. But there's a form of law in Doctors-Common and I swear, sister Sullen, rather than see you this continually discontented, I would advise you apply to that: for besides the part that I bear your vexatious broils, as being sister to the husband and friend to the wife, your example gives me such an impression of matrimony, that I shall be apt condemn my person to a long vacation all its life But supposing, madam, that you brought it to case of separation, what can you urge against your husband? My brother is, first, the most constant man alive.

Mrs. Sul. The most constant husband, I grant ye.

Dor. He never sleeps from you.

Mrs. Sul. No, he always sleeps with me.

Dor. He allows you a maintenance suitable to your quality.

Mrs. Sul. A maintenance! do you take me, madam, for an hospital child, that I must sit down, and bless my benefactors for meat, drink, and clothes? As I take it, madam, I brought your brother ten thousand pounds, out of which I might expect some pretty things, called pleasures.

Dor. You share in all the pleasures that the country affords.

Mrs. Sul. Country pleasures! racks and torments! Dost think, child, that my limbs were made for leaping of ditches, and clambering over stiles?

or that my parents, wisely foreseeing my future happiness in country pleasures, had early instructed me in rural accomplishments of drinking fat ale, playing at whisk, and smoking tobacco with my husband? or of spreading of plasters, brewing of diet-drinks, and stilling rosemary-water, with the good old gentlewoman my mother-in-law?

Dor. I'm sorry, madam, that it is not more in our power to divert you; I could wish, indeed, that our entertainments were a little more polite, or your taste a little less refined. But, pray, madam, how came the poets and philosophers, that laboured so much in hunting after pleasure, to place it at last in a country life?

Mrs. Sul. Because they wanted money, child, to find out the pleasures of the town. Did you ever see a poet or philosopher worth ten thousand pounds? if you can show me such a man, I 'll lay you fifty pounds you'll find him somewhere within the weekly bills. Not that I disapprove rural pleasures, as the poets have painted them; in their landscape, every Phillis has her Corydon, every murmuring stream, and every flowery mead, gives fresh alarms to love. Besides, you'll find, that their couples were never married:—but yonder I see my Corydon, and a sweet swain it is, Heaven knows! Come, Dorinda, don't be angry, he's my husband, and your brother; and, between both, is he not a sad brute?

Dor. I have nothing to say to your part of him, you 're the best judge.

Mrs. Sul. O sister, sister! if ever you marry, beware of a sullen, silent sot, one that's always musing, but never thinks. There's some diversion in a talking blockhead; and since a woman must wear chains, I would have the pleasure of hearing 'em rattle a little. Now you shall see, but take this by the way. He came home this morning at his usual hour of four, wakened me out of a sweet dream of something else, by tumbling over the tea-table, which he broke all to pieces; after his man and he had rolled about the room, like sick passengers in a storm, he comes flounce into bed, dead as a salmon into a fishmonger's basket; his feet cold as ice, his breath hot as a furnace, and his hands and his face as greasy as his flannel night-cap. O matrimony! He tosses up the clothes with a barbarous swing over his shoulders, disorders the whole economy of my bed, leaves me half naked, and my whole night's comfort is the tuneable serenade of that wakeful nightingale, his nose! Oh, the pleasure of counting the melancholy clock by a snoring husband! But now, sister, you shall see how handsomely, being a well-bred man, he will beg my pardon.

Enter Squire Sullen.

Squire Sul. My head aches consumedly.
Mrs. Sul. Will you be pleased, my dear, to drink tea with us this morning? it may do your head good.
Squire Sul. No.
Dor. Coffee, brother?
Squire Sul. Psha!
Mrs. Sul. Will you please to dress, and go to church with me? the air may help you.
Squire Sul. Scrub! [*Calls.*

Enter Scrub.

Scrub. Sir!
Squire Sul. What day o' th' week is this?
Scrub. Sunday, an't please your worship.
Squire Sul. Sunday! bring me a dram; and d'ye hear, set out the venison-pasty, and a tankard of strong beer upon the hall-table, I 'll go to breakfast [*Going.*
Dor. Stay, stay, brother, you shan't get off so; you were very naught last night, and must make your wife reparation; come, come, brother, won't you ask pardon?
Squire Sul. For what?
Dor. For being drunk last night.

Squire Sul. I can afford it, can't I?

Mrs. Sul. But I can't, sir.

Squire Sul. Then you may let it alone.

Mrs. Sul. But I must tell you, sir, that this is not to be borne.

Squire Sul. I 'm glad on't.

Mrs. Sul. What is the reason, sir, that you use me thus inhumanly?

Squire Sul. Scrub!

Scrub. Sir!

Squire Sul. Get things ready to shave my head. [*Exit.*

Mrs. Sul. Have a care of coming near his temples, Scrub, for fear you meet something there that may turn the edge of your razor.—[*Exit Scrub.*] Inveterate stupidity I did you ever know so hard, so obstinate a spleen as his? O sister, sister! I shall never ha' good of the beast till I get him to town; London, dear London, is the place for managing and breaking a husband.

Dor. And has not a husband the same opportunities there for humbling a wife?

Mrs. Sul. No, no, child, 'tis a standing maxim in conjugal discipline, that when a man would enslave his wife, he hurries her into the country; and when a lady would be arbitrary with her husband, she wheedles her booby up to town. A man dare not play the tyrant in London, because there are so many examples to encourage the subject to rebel. O Dorinda! Dorinda! a fine woman may do anything in London: o' my conscience, she may raise an army of forty thousand men.

Dor. I fancy, sister, you have a mind to be trying your power that way here in Lichfield; you have drawn the French count to your colours already.

Mrs. Sul. The French are a people that can't live without their gallantries.

Dor. And some English that I know, sister, are not averse to such amusements.

Mrs. Sul. Well, sister, since the truth must out, it may do as well now as hereafter; I think, one way to rouse my lethargic, sottish husband, is to give him a rival: security begets negligence in all people, and men must be alarmed to make 'em alert-in their duty. Women are

41

like pictures, of no value in the hands of a fool, till he hears men of sense bid high for the purchase.

Dor. This might do, sister, if my brother's understanding were to be convinced into a passion for you; but, I fancy, there's a natural aversion on his side; and I fancy, sister, that you don't come much behind him, if you dealt fairly.

Mrs. Sul. I own it, we are united contradictions, fire and water: but I could be contented, with a great many other wives, to humour the censorious mob, and give the world an appearance of living well with my husband, could I bring him but to dissemble a little kindness to keep me in countenance.

Dor. But how do you know, sister, but that, instead of rousing your husband by this artifice to a counterfeit kindness, he should awake in a real fury?

Mrs. Sul. Let him: if I can't entice him to the one, I would provoke him to the other.

Dor. But how must I behave myself between ye?

Mrs. Sul. You must assist me.

Dor. What, against my own brother?

Mrs. Sul. He's but half a brother, and I 'm your entire friend. If I go a step beyond the bounds of honour, leave me; till then, I expect you should go along with me in everything; while I trust my honour in your hands, you may trust your brother's in mine. The count is to dine here to-day.

Dor. 'Tis a strange thing, sister, that I can't like that man.

Mrs. Sul. You like nothing; your time is not come; Love and Death have their fatalities, and strike home one time or other: you 'll pay for all one day, I warrant ye. But come, my lady's tea is ready, and 'tis almost church time. [*Exeunt.*

ACT II., SCENE II.

A Room in Boniface's Inn. Enter Aimwell dressed, and Archer.

Aim. And was she the daughter of the house?

Arch. The landlord is so blind as to think so; but I dare swear she has better blood in her veins.

Aim. Why dost think so?

Arch. Because the baggage has a pert *je ne sais quoi*; she reads plays, keeps a monkey, and is troubled with vapours.

Aim. By which discoveries I guess that you know more of *Cher.*

Arch. Not yet, faith; the lady gives herself airs; forsooth, nothing under a gentleman!

Aim. Let me take her in hand.

Arch. Say one word more of that, and I'll declare myself, spoil your sport there, and everywhere else; look ye, Aim well, every man in his own sphere.

Aim. Right; and therefore you must pimp for your master.

Arch. In the usual forms, good sir, after I have served myself.—But to our business. You are so well dressed, Tom, and make so handsome a figure, that I fancy you may do execution in a country church; the exterior part strikes first, and you're in the right to make that impression favourable.

Aim. There's something in that which may turn to advantage. The appearance of a stranger in a country church draws as many gazers as a blazing-star; no sooner he comes into the cathedral, but a train of whispers runs buzzing round the congregation in a moment:

Who is he? Whence comes he? Do you know him? Then I, sir, tips me the verger with half-a-crown; he pockets the simony, and inducts me into the best pew in the church; I pull out my snuff-box, turn myself round, bow to the bishop, or the dean, if he be the commanding-officer; single out a beauty, rivet both my eyes to hers, set my nose a-bleeding by the strength of imagination, and show the whole church my concern, by my endeavouring to hide it; after the sermon, the whole town gives me to her for a lover, and by persuading the lady that I am a-dying for her, the tables are turned, and she in good earnest falls in love with me.

Arch. There's nothing in this, Tom, without a precedent; but instead of riveting your eyes to a beauty, try to fix 'em upon a fortune; that's our business at present.

Aim. Psha! no woman can be a beauty without a fortune. Let me alone, for I am a marksman.

Arch. Tom!

Aim. Ay.

Arch. When were you at church before, pray?

Aim. Um—I was there at the coronation.

Arch. And how can you expect a blessing by going to church now?

Aim. Blessing! nay, Frank, I ask but for a wife. [*Exit.*

Arch. Truly, the man is not very unreasonable in his demands. [*Exit at the opposite door.*

Enter Boniface and Cherry.

Bon. Well, daughter, as the saying is, have you brought Martin to confess?

Cher. Pray, father, don't put me upon getting anything out of a man; I 'm but young, you know, father, and I don't understand wheedling.

Bon. Young! why, you jade, as the saying is, can any woman wheedle that is not young? your mother was useless at five-and-twenty. Not wheedle!

would you make your mother a whore, and me a cuckold, as the saying is? I tell you, his silence confesses it, and his master spends his money so freely, and is so much a gentleman every manner of way, that he must be a highwayman.

Enter Gibbet, in a cloak.

Gib. Landlord, landlord, is the coast clear?

Bon. O Mr. Gibbet, what 's the news?

Gib. No matter, ask no questions, all fair and honourable.—Here, my dear Cherry.—[*Gives her a bag.*] Two hundred sterling pounds, as good as any that ever hanged or saved a rogue; lay 'em by with the rest; and here-three wedding or mourning rings, 'tis much the same you know-here, two silver-hilted swords; I took those from fellows that never show any part of their swords but the hilts-here is a diamond necklace which the lady hid in the privatest place in the coach, but I found it out—this gold watch I took from a pawnbroker's wife; it was left in her hands by a person of quality: there's the arms upon the case.

Cher. But who had you the money from?

Gib. Ah! poor woman! I pitied her;-from a poor lady just eloped from her husband. She had made up her cargo, and was bound for Ireland, as hard as she could drive; she told me of her husband's barbarous usage, and so I left her half-a-crown. But I had almost forgot, my dear Cherry, I have a present for you.

Cher. What is 't?

Gib. A pot of ceruse, my child, that I took out of a lady's under-pocket.

Cher. What, Mr. Gibbet, do you think that I paint?

Gib. Why, you jade, your betters do; I 'm sure the lady that I took it from had a coronet upon her handkerchief. Here, take my cloak, and go, secure the premises.

Cher. I will secure 'em. [*Exit.*

Bon. But, hark'ee, where's Hounslow and Bagshot?

Gib. They'll be here to-night.

Bon. D' ye know of any other gentlemen o' the pad on this road?

Gib. No.

Bon. I fancy that I have two that lodge in the house just now.

Gib. The devil! how d'ye smoke 'em?

Bon. Why, the one is gone to church.

Gib. That's suspicious, I must confess.

Bon. And the other is now in his master's chamber; he pretends to be servant to the other; we 'll call him out and pump him a little.

Gib. With all my heart.

Bon. Mr. Martin! Mr. Martin! [*Calls.*

Enter Archer, combing a periwig and singing.

Gib. The roads are consumed deep, I'm as dirty as Old Brentford at Christmas.—A good pretty fellow that; whose servant are you, friend?

Arch. My master's.

Gib. Really!

Arch. Really.

Gib. That 's much.—The fellow has been at the bar by his evasions.— But, pray, sir, what is your master's name?

Arch. Tall, all, dall!—[*Sings and combs the periwig.*] This is the most obstinate curl—

Gib. I ask you his name?

Arch. Name, sir—*tall, all, doll!*—I never asked him his name in my life.— *Tall, all, doll!*

Bon. What think you now? [*Aside to Gibbet.*

Gib. [*Aside to Boniface.*] Plain, plain, he talks now as if he were before a judge.—[*To Archer.*] But pray, friend, which way does your master travel?

Arch. A-horseback.

Gib. [*Aside.*] Very well again, an old offender, right—

[*To Archer.*] But, I mean, does he go upwards or downwards?

Arch. Downwards, I fear, sir.—*Tall, all!*

Gib. I 'm afraid my fate will be a contrary way.

Bon. Ha! ha! ha! Mr. Martin, you 're very arch. This gentleman is only travelling towards Chester, and would be glad of your company, that's all.—Come, captain, you'll stay to-night, I suppose? I'll show you a chamber—come, captain.

Gib. Farewell, friend!

Arch. Captain, your servant.—[*Exeunt Boniface and Gibbet.*] Captain! a pretty fellow! 'Sdeath, I wonder that the officers of the army don't conspire to beat all scoundrels in red but their own.

Re-enter Cherry.

Cher. [*Aside.*] Gone, and Martin here! I hope he did not listen; I would have the merit of the discovery all my own, because I would oblige him to love me.—[*Aloud*] Mr. Martin, who was that man with my father?

Arch. Some recruiting Serjeant, or whipped-out trooper, I suppose.

Cher. All's safe, I find. [*Aside*

Arch. Come, my dear, have you conned over the catechise I taught you last night?

Cher. Come, question me.

Arch. What is love?

Cher. Love is I know not what, it comes I know not how, and goes I know not when.

Arch. Very well, an apt scholar.—[*Chucks her under the chin.*] Where does love enter?

Cher. Into the eyes.

Arch. And where go out?

Cher. I won't tell ye.

Arch. What are the objects of that passion?

Cher. Youth, beauty, and clean linen.

Arch. The reason?

Cher. The two first are fashionable in nature, and the third at court.

Arch. That's my dear.—What are the signs and tokens of that passion?

Cher. A stealing look, a stammering tongue, words improbable, designs impossible, and actions impracticable.

Arch. That's my good child, kiss me.—-What must a lover do to obtain his mistress?

Cher. He must adore the person that disdains him, he must bribe the chambermaid that betrays him, and court the footman that laughs at him. He must—he must—

Arch. Nay, child, I must whip you if you don't mind your lesson; he must treat his—

Cher. Oh ay!—he must treat his enemies with respect, his friends with indifference, and all the world with contempt; he must suffer much, and fear more; he must desire much, and hope little; in short, he must embrace his ruin, and throw himself away.

Arch. Had ever man so hopeful a pupil as mine!—Come, my dear, why is love called a riddle?

Cher. Because, being blind, he leads those that see, and, though a child, he governs a man.

Arch. Mighty well!—And why is Love pictured blind?

Cher. Because the painters out of the weakness or privilege of their art chose to hide those eyes that they could not draw.

Arch. That's my dear little scholar, kiss me again.—And why should Love, that's a child, govern a man?

Cher. Because that a child is the end of love.

Arch. And so ends Love's catechism.—And now, my dear, we'll go in and make my master's bed.

Cher. Hold, hold, Mr. Martin! You have taken a great deal of pains to instruct me, and what d' ye think I have learned by it?

Arch. What?

Cher. That your discourse and your habit are contradictions, and it would be nonsense in me to believe you a footman any longer.

Arch. 'Oons, what a witch it is!

Cher. Depend upon this, sir, nothing in this garb shall ever tempt me; for, though I was born to servitude, I hate it. Own your condition, swear you love me, and then—

Arch. And then we shall go make my master's bed?

Cher. Yes.

Arch. You must know, then, that I am born a gentleman, my education was liberal; but I went to London a younger brother, fell into the hands of sharpers, who stripped me of my money, my friends disowned me, and now my necessity brings me to what you see.

Cher. Then take my hand—promise to marry me before you sleep, and I'll make you master of two thousand pounds.

Arch. How!

Cher. Two thousand pounds that I have this minute in my own custody; so, throw off your livery this instant, and I 'll go find a parson.

Arch. What said you? a parson!

Cher. What! do you scruple?

Arch. Scruple! no, no, but—Two thousand pounds, you say?

Cher. And better.

Arch. [*Aside.*] 'Sdeath, what shall I do?—[*Aloud.*] But hark 'ee, child, what need you make me master of yourself and money, when you may have the same pleasure out of me, and still keep your fortune in your hands?

Cher. Then you won't marry me?

Arch. I would marry you, but—

Cher. O sweet sir, I'm your humble servant, you're fairly caught! Would you persuade me that any gentleman who could bear the scandal of wearing a livery would refuse two thousand pounds, let the condition be what it would? no, no, sir. But I hope you 'll pardon the freedom I have taken, since it was only to inform myself of the respect that I ought to pay you. [*Going.*

Arch. [*Aside.*] Fairly bit, by Jupiter!—[*Aloud.*] Hold! hold!—And have you actually two thousand pounds?

Cher. Sir, I have my secrets as well as you; when you please to be more open I shall be more free, and be assured that I have discoveries that will match yours, be what they will. In the meanwhile, be satisfied that no discovery I make shall ever hurt you, but beware of my father! [*Exit.*

Arch. So! we're like to have as many adventures in our inn as Don Quixote had in his. Let me see—two thousand pounds—if the wench would promise to die when the money were spent, egad, one would marry her; but the fortune may go off in a year or two, and the wife may live—Lord knows how long. Then an innkeeper's daughter! ay, that's the devil—there my pride brings me off.

For whatsoe'er the sages charge on pride, The angels' fall, and twenty faults beside, On earth, I'm sure, 'mong us of mortal calling, Pride saves man oft, and woman too, from falling.

[*Exit.*

ACT III., SCENE I

The Gallery in Lady Bountiful's House. Enter Mrs. Sullen and Dorinda.

Mrs. Su., Ha! ha! ha! my dear sister, let me embrace thee! now we are friends indeed; for I shall have a secret of yours as a pledge for mine—now you'll be good for something, I shall have you conversable in the subjects of the sex.

Dor. But do you think that I am so weak as to fall in love with a fellow at first sight?

Mrs. Sul. Psha! now you spoil all; why should not we be as free in our friendships as the men? I warrant you, the gentleman has got to his confidant already, has avowed his passion, toasted your health, called you ten thousand angels, has run over your lips, eyes, neck, shape, air, and everything, in a description that warms their mirth to a second enjoyment.

Dor. Your hand, sister, I an't well.

Mrs. Sul. So—she's breeding already—come, child, up with it—hem a little—so—now tell me, don't you like the gentleman that we saw at church just now?

Dor. The man's well enough.

Mrs. Sul. Well enough! is he not a demigod, a Narcissus, a star, the man i' the moon?

Dor. O sister, I'm extremely ill!

Mrs. Sul. Shall I send to your mother, child, for a little of her cephalic plaster to put to the soles of your feet, or shall I send to the gentleman for something for you? Come, unlace your stays, unbosom yourself.

The man is perfectly a pretty fellow; I saw him when he first came into church.

Dor. I saw him too, sister, and with an air that shone, methought, like rays about his person.

Mrs. Sul. Well said, up with it!

Dor. No forward coquette behaviour, no airs to set him off, no studied looks nor artful posture—but Nature did it all—

Mrs. Sul. Better and better!—one touch more—come!

Dor. But then his looks—did you observe his eyes?

Mrs. Sul. Yes, yes, I did.—His eyes, well, what of his eyes?

Dor. Sprightly, but not wandering; they seemed to view, but never gazed on anything but me.—And then his looks so humble were, and yet so noble, that they aimed to tell me that he could with pride die at my feet, though he scorned slavery anywhere else.

Mrs. Sul. The physic works purely!—How d' ye find yourself now, my dear?

Dor. Hem! much better, my dear.—Oh, here comes our Mercury!

Enter Scrub.

Well, Scrub, what news of the gentleman?

Scrub. Madam, I have brought you a packet of news.

Dor. Open it quickly, come.

Scrub. In the first place I inquired who the gentleman was; they told me he was a stranger. Secondly, I asked what the gentleman was; they answered and said, that they never saw him before. Thirdly, I inquired what countryman he was; they replied, 'twas more than they knew. Fourthly, I demanded whence he came; their answer was, they could not tell. And, fifthly, I asked whither he went; and they replied, they knew nothing of the matter,—and this is all I could learn.

Mrs. Sul. But what do the people say? can't they guess?

Scrub. Why, some think he's a spy, some guess he's a mountebank, some say one thing, some another: but, for my own part, I believe he's a Jesuit.

Dor. A Jesuit! why a Jesuit?

Scrub. Because he keeps his horses always ready saddled, and his footman talks French.

Mrs. Sul. His footman!

Scrub. Ay, he and the count's footman were jabbering French like two intriguing ducks in a mill-pond; and I believe they talked of me, for they laughed consumedly.

Dor. What sort of livery has the footman?

Scrub. Livery! Lord, madam, I took him for a captain, he's so bedizzened with lace! And then he has tops to his shoes, up to his mid leg, a silver-headed cane dangling at his knuckles; he carries his hands in his pockets just so—[*walks in the French air.*—and has a fine long periwig tied up in a bag.—Lord, madam, he's clear another sort of man than I!

Mrs. Sul. That may easily be.—But what shall we do now, sister?

Dor. I have it—this fellow has a world of simplicity, and some cunning, the first hides the latter by abundance.—Scrub!

Scrub. Madam!

Dor. We have a great mind to know who this gentleman is, only for our satisfaction.

Scrub. Yes, madam, it would be a satisfaction, no doubt.

Dor. You must go and get acquainted with his footman, and invite him hither to drink a bottle of your ale because you 're butler to-day.

Scrub. Yes, madam, I am butler every Sunday.

Mrs. Sul. O' brave! sister, o' my conscience, you understand the mathematics already. 'Tis the best plot in the world: your mother, you know, will be gone to church, my spouse will be got to the ale-house with his scoundrels, and the house will be our own—so we drop in by accident, and ask the fellow some questions ourselves.

In the country, you know, any stranger is company, and we're glad to take up with the butler in a country-dance, and happy if he 'll do us the favour.

Scrub. O madam, you wrong me! I never refused your ladyship the favour in my life.

Enter Gipsy.

Gip. Ladies, dinner's upon table.

Dor. Scrub, we'll excuse your waiting—go where we ordered you.

Scrub. I shall. [*Exeunt.*

ACT III., SCENE II

A Room in Bonifaces Inn. Enter Aimwell and Archer.

Arch. Well, Tom, I find you 're a marksman.

Aim. A marksman! who so blind could be, as not discern a swan among the ravens?

Arch. Well, but hark'ee, Aimwell!

Aim. Aimwell! call me Oroondates, Cesario, Amadis, all that romance can in a lover paint, and then I 'll answer. O Archer! I read her thousands in her looks, she looked like Ceres in her harvest: corn, wine and oil, milk and honey, gardens, groves, and purling streams played on her plenteous face.

Arch. Her face! her pocket, you mean; the corn, wine and oil, lies there. In short, she has ten thousand pounds, that's the English on't.

Aim. Her eyes—

Arch. Are demi-cannons, to be sure; so I won't stand their battery. [*Going.*

Aim.-Pray excuse me, my passion must have vent.

Arch. Passion! what a plague, d' ye think these romantic airs will do our business? Were my temper as extravagant as yours, my adventures have something more romantic by half.

Aim. Your adventures!

Arch. Yes,

> *The nymph that with her twice ten hundred pounds,*
> *With brazen engine hot, and quoif clear-starched,*

Can fire the guest in warming of the bed—

There's a touch of sublime Milton for you, and the subject but an innkeeper's daughter! I can play with a girl as an angler does with his fish; he keeps it at the end of his line, runs it up the stream, and down the stream, till at last he brings it to hand, tickles the trout, and so whips it into his basket.

Enter Boniface.

Bon. Mr. Martin, as the saying is—yonder's an honest fellow below, my Lady Bountiful's butler, who begs the honour that you would go home with him and see his cellar.

Arch. Do my *baise-mains* to the gentleman, and tell him I will do myself the honour to wait on him immediately. [*Exit Boniface.*

Aim. What do I hear? Soft Orpheus play, and fair Toftida sing!

Arch. Psha! damn your raptures; I tell you, here's a pump going to be put into the vessel, and the ship will get into harbour, my life on't. You say, there's another lady very handsome there?

Aim. Yes, faith.

Arch. I 'm in love with her already.

Aim. Can't you give me a bill upon Cherry in the meantime?

Arch. No, no, friend, all her corn, wine and oil, is ingrossed to my market. And once more I warn you, to keep your anchorage clear of mine; for if you fall foul of me, by this light you shall go to the bottom! What! make prize of my little frigate, while I am upon the cruise for you!—

Aim. Well, well, I won't. [*Exit Archer.*

Re-enter Boniface.

Landlord, have you any tolerable company in the house, I don't care for dining alone?

Bon. Yes, sir, there's a captain below, as the saying is, that arrived about an hour ago.

Aim. Gentlemen of his coat are welcome everywhere; will you make him a compliment from me and tell him I should be glad of his company?

Bon. Who shall I tell him, sir, would—

Aim. [*Aside.*] Ha! that stroke was well thrown in!—

[*Aloud.*] I'm only a traveller, like himself, and would be glad of his company, that's all.

Bon. I obey your commands, as the saying is. [*Exit.*

Re-enter Archer.

Arch. 'Sdeath I I had forgot; what title will you give yourself?

Aim. My brother's, to be sure; he would never give me anything else, so I'll make bold with his honour this bout:—you know the rest of your cue.

Arch. Ay, ay. [*Exit.*

Enter Gibbet.

Gib. Sir, I 'm yours.

Aim. 'Tis more than I deserve, sir, for I don't know you.

Gib. I don't wonder at that, sir, for you never saw me before—[*Aside*] I hope.

Aim. And pray, sir, how came I by the honour of seeing you now?

Gib. Sir, I scorn to intrude upon any gentleman—but my landlord—

Aim. O sir, I ask your pardon, you 're the captain he told me of?

Gib. At your service, sir.

Aim. What regiment, may I be so bold?

Gib. A marching regiment, sir, an old corps.

Aim. [*Aside.*] Very old, if your coat be regimental—[*Aloud.*] You have served abroad, sir?

Gib. Yes, sir—in the plantations, 'twas my lot to be sent into the worst service; I would have quitted it indeed, but a man of honour, you know—Besides, 'twas for the good of my country that I should be abroad:—anything for the good of one's country—I'm a Roman for that.

Aim. [*Aside.*] One of the first; I 'll lay my life. [*Aloud.*] You found the West Indies very hot, sir?

Gib. Ay, sir, too hot for me.

Aim. Pray, sir, han't I seen your face at Will's coffee-house?

Gib. Yes, sir, and at White's too.

Aim. And where is your company now, captain?

Gib. They an't come yet.

Aim. Why, d' ye expect 'em here?

Gib. They 'll be here to-night, sir.

Aim. Which way do they march?

Gib. Across the country.—[*Aside.*] The devil's in 't, if I han't said enough to encourage him to declare! But I'm afraid he's not right; I must tack about

Aim. Is your company to quarter in Lichfield?

Gib. In this house, sir.

Aim. What! all?

Gib. My company's but thin, ha! ha! ha! we are but three, ha! ha! ha!

Aim. You're merry, sir.

Gib. Ay, sir, you must excuse me, sir; I understand the world, especially the art of travelling: I don't care, sir, for answering questions directly upon the road—for I generally ride with a charge about me.

Aim. Three or four, I believe. [Aside.

Gib. I am credibly informed that there are highwaymen upon this quarter; not, sir, that I could suspect a gentleman of your figure—but truly, sir, I have got such a way of evasion upon the road, that I don't care for speaking truth to any man.

Aim. [*Aside.*] Your caution may be necessary.—[*Aloud.*] Then I presume you're no captain?

Gib. Not I, sir; captain is a good travelling name, and so I take it; it stops a great many foolish inquiries that are generally made about gentlemen that travel, it gives a man an air of something, and makes the drawers obedient:—and thus far I am a captain, and no farther.

Aim. And pray, sir, what is your true profession?

Gib. O sir, you must excuse me!—upon my word, sir, I don't think it safe to tell ye.

Aim. Ha! ha! ha! upon my word I commend you.

Re-enter Boniface.

Well, Mr. Boniface, what's the news?

Bon. There's another gentleman below, as the saying is, that hearing you were but two, would be glad to make the third man, if you would give him leave.

Aim. What is he?

Bon. A clergyman, as the saying is.

Aim. A clergyman! is he really a clergyman? or is it only his travelling name, as my friend the captain has it?

Bon. O sir, he's a priest, and chaplain to the French officers in town.

Aim. Is he a Frenchman?

Bon. Yes, sir, born at Brussels.

Gib. A Frenchman, and a priest! I won't be seen in his company, sir; I have a value for my reputation, sir.

Aim. Nay, but, captain, since we are by ourselves—can he speak English, landlord?

Bon. Very well, sir; you may know him, as the saying is, to be a foreigner by his accent, and that's all.

Aim. Then he has been in England before?

Bon. Never, sir; but he's a master of languages, as the saying is; he talks Latin—it does me good to hear him talk Latin.

Aim. Then you understand Latin, Mr Boniface?

Bon. Not I, sir, as the saying is; but he talks it so very fast, that I 'm sure it must be good.

Aim. Pray, desire him to walk up.

Bon. Here he is, as the saying is.

Enter Foigard.

Foi. Save you, gentlemens, bote.

Aim. [*Aside.*] A Frenchman!—[To Foigard.] Sir, your most humble servant.

Foi. Och, dear joy, I am your most faithful shervant, and yours alsho.

Gib. Doctor, you talk very good English, but you have a mighty twang of the foreigner.

Foi. My English is very veil for the vords, but we foreigners, you know, cannot bring our tongues about the pronunciation so soon.

Aim. [*Aside.*] A foreigner! a downright Teague, by this light!—[*Aloud.*] Were you born in France, doctor?

Foi. I was educated in France, but I was borned at Brussels; I am a subject of the King of Spain, joy.

Gib. What King of Spain, sir? speak!

Foi. Upon my shoul, joy, I cannot tell you as yet.

Aim. Nay, captain, that was too hard upon the doctor; he's a stranger.

Foi. Oh, let him alone, dear joy; I am of a nation that is not easily put out of countenance.

Aim. Come, gentlemen, I 'll end the dispute.—Here, landlord, is dinner ready?

Bon. Upon the table, as the saying is.

Aim. Gentlemen—pray—that door—

Foi. No, no, fait, the captain must lead.

Aim. No, doctor, the church is our guide.

Gib. Ay, ay, so it is.

[*Exit Foigard foremost, the others following.*

ACT III., SCENE III.

The Gallery in Lady Bountiful's House.

Enter Archer and Scrub singing, and hugging one another, the latter with a tankard in his hand Gipsy listening at a distance.

Scrub. Tall, all, dall!—Come, my dear boy, let 's have that song once more.

Arch. No, no, we shall disturb the family.—But will you be sure to keep the secret?

Scrub. Pho! upon my honour, as I'm a gentleman.

Arch. 'Tis enough. You must know, then, that my master is the Lord Viscount Aimwell; he fought a duel t' other day in London, wounded his man so dangerously, that he thinks fit to withdraw till he hears whether the gentleman's wounds be mortal or not He never was in this part of England before, so he chose to retire to this place, that's all.

Gip. And that's enough for me. [*Exit.*

Scrub. And where were you when your master fought?

Arch. We never know of our masters' quarrels.

Scrub. No! if our masters in the country here receive a challenge, the first thing they do is to tell their wives; the wife tells the servants, the servants alarm the tenants, and in half an hour you shall have the whole county in arms.

Arch. To hinder two men from doing what they have no mind for.—But if you should chance to talk now of my business?

Scrub. Talk! ay, sir, had I not learned the knack of holding my tongue, I had never lived so long in a great family.

Arch. Ay, ay, to be sure there are secrets in all families.

Scrub. Secrets! ay;—but I 'll say no more. Come, sit down, we 'll make an end of our tankard: here—

[*Gives Archer the tankard.*

Arch. With all my heart; who knows but you and I may come to be better acquainted, eh? Here's your ladies' healths; you have three, I think, and to be sure there must be secrets among 'em. [*Drinks.*

Scrub. Secrets! ay, friend.—I wish I had a friend!

Arch. Am not I your friend? come, you and I will sworn brothers.

Scrub. Shall we?

Arch. . From this minute. Give me a kiss:—and no brother Scrub—

Scrub. And now, brother Martin, I will tell you a secret that will make your hair stand on end. You must know that I am consumedly in love.

Arch. That's a terrible secret, that's the truth on't

Scrub. That jade, Gipsy, that was with us just now in the cellar, is the arrantest whore that ever wore a petticoat; and I 'm dying for love of her.

Arch. Ha! ha! ha!—Are you in love with her person her virtue, brother Scrub?

Scrub. I should like virtue best, because it is more durable than beauty: for virtue holds good with some women long, and many a day after they have lost it.

Arch. In the country, I grant ye, where no woman's virtue is lost, till a bastard be found.

Scrub. Ay, could I bring her to a bastard, I should have her all to myself; but I dare not put it upon, the lay, for fear of being sent for a soldier. Pray brother, how do you gentlemen in London like this same Pressing Act?

62

Arch. Very ill, brother Scrub; 'tis the worst that ever was made for us. Formerly I remember the good days, when we could dun our masters for our wage and if they refused to pay us, we could have a warrant to carry 'em before a Justice: but now if we talk of eating, they have a warrant for us, and carry us before three Justices.

Scrub. And to be sure we go, if we talk of eating; for the Justices won't give their own servants a bad example. Now this is my misfortune—I dare not speak in the house, while that jade Gipsy dings about like a fury.——Once I had the better end of the staff.

Arch. And how comes the change now?

Scrub. Why, the mother of all this mischief is a priest.

Arch. A priest!

Scrub. Ay, a damned son of a whore of Babylon, that came over hither to say grace to the French officers, and eat up our provisions. There's not a day goes over his head without a dinner or supper in this house.

Arch. How came he so familiar in the family?

Scrub. Because he speaks English as if he had lived here all his life, and tells lies as if he had been a traveller from his cradle.

Arch. And this priest, I'm afraid, has converted the affections of your Gipsy?

Scrub. Converted! ay, and perverted, my dear friend: for, I 'm afraid, he has made her a whore and a papist! But this is not all; there's the French count and Mrs. Sullen, they 're in the confederacy, and for some private ends of their own, to be sure.

Arch. A very hopeful family yours, brother Scrub! suppose the maiden lady has her lover too?

Scrub. Not that I know: she's the best on 'em, that's the truth on't: but they take care to prevent my curiosity, by giving me so much business, that I'm a perfect slave. What d' ye think is my place in this family?

Arch. Butler, I suppose.

Scrub. Ah, Lord help you! I 'll tell you. Of a Monday I drive the coach, of a Tuesday I drive the plough, on Wednesday I follow the hounds, a Thursday I dun the tenants, on Friday I go to market, on Saturday I draw warrants, and a Sunday I draw beer.

Arch. Ha! ha! ha! if variety be a pleasure in life, you have enough on't, my dear brother. But what ladies are those?

Scrub. Ours, ours; that upon the right hand is Mrs. Sullen, and the other is Mrs. Dorinda. Don't mind 'em; sit still, man.

Enter Mrs. Sullen and Dorinda.

Mrs. Sul. I have heard my brother talk of my Lord Aimwell; but they say that his brother is the finer gentleman.

Dor. That's impossible, sister.

Mrs. Sul. He's vastly rich, but very close, they say.

Dor. No matter for that; if I can creep into his heart, I 'll open his breast, I warrant him: I have heard say, that people may be guessed at by the behaviour of their servants; I could wish we might talk to that fellow.

Mrs. Sul. So do I; for I think he 's a very pretty fellow. Come this way, I'll throw out a lure for him presently.

[*Dorinda and Mrs. Sullen walk a turn towards the opposite side of the stage.*

Arch. [*Aside.*] Corn, wine, and oil indeed!—But, I think, the wife has the greatest plenty of flesh and blood; she should be my choice.—Ay, ay, say you so!—[*Mrs. Sullen drops her glove. Archer runs, takes it up and gives to her.*] Madam—your ladyship's glove.

Mrs. Sul. O sir, I thank you!—[To Dorinda.] What a handsome bow the fellow has!

Dor. Bow! why, I have known several footmen come down from London set up here for dancing-masters, and carry off the best fortunes in the country.

Arch. [*Aside.*] That project, for aught I know, had been better than ours.— [*To Scrub.*] Brother Scrub, why don't you introduce me?

Scrub. Ladies, this is the strange gentleman's servant that you saw at church to-day; I understood he came from London, and so I invited him to the cellar, that he might show me the newest flourish in whetting my knives.

Dor. And I hope you have made much of him?

Arch. Oh yes, madam, but the strength of your lady ship's liquor is a little too potent for the constitution of your humble servant.

Mrs. Sul. What, then you don't usually drink ale?

Arch. No, madam; my constant drink is tea, or a little wine and water. 'Tis prescribed me by the physician for a remedy against the spleen.

Scrub. Oh la! Oh la! a footman have the spleen!

Mrs. Sul. I thought that distemper had been only proper to people of quality?

Arch. Madam, like all other fashions it wears Out, and so descends to their servants; though in a great many of us, I believe, it proceeds from some melancholy particles in the blood, occasioned by the stagnation of wages.

Dor. [*Aside to Mrs. Sullen.*] How affectedly the fello* talks!—[*To Archer.*] How long, pray, have yon served your present master?

Arch. Not long; my life has been mostly spent in the service of the ladies.

Mrs. Sul. And pray, which service do you like best?

Arch. Madam, the ladies pay best; the honour of serving them is sufficient wages; there is a charm in their looks that delivers a pleasure with their commands, and gives our duty the wings of inclination.

Mrs. Sul. [*Aside.*] That flight was above the pitch of a livery.—[*Aloud.*] And, sir, would not you be satisfied to serve a lady again?

Arch. As a groom of the chamber, madam, but not as a footman.

Mrs. Sul. I suppose you served as footman before? *Arch.* For that reason
I would not serve in that post again; for my memory is too weak
for the load of messages that the ladies lay upon their servants in
London. My Lady Howd'ye, the last mistress I served, called me up
one morning, and told me, 'Martin, go to my Lady Allnight with my
humble service; tell her I was to wait on her ladyship yesterday, and
left word with Mrs. Rebecca, that the preliminaries of the affair she
knows of, are stopped till we know the concurrence of the person
that I know of, for which there are circumstances wanting which we
shall accommodate at the old place; but that in the meantime there
is a person about her ladyship, that from several hints and surmises,
was accessory at a certain time to the disappointments that naturally
attend things, that to her knowledge are of more importance—'

Mrs. Sul., Dor. Ha! ha! ha! where are you going, sir?

Arch. Why, I han't half done!—The whole howd'ye was about half an
hour long; so I happened to misplace two syllables, and was turned
off, and rendered incapable.

Dor. [*Aside to Mrs. Sullen.*] The pleasantest fellow, sister, I ever saw!—[*To
Archer.*] But, friend, if your master be married, I presume you still
serve a lady?

Arch. No, madam, I take care never to come into a married family; the
commands of the master and mistress are always so contrary, that
'tis impossible to please both.

Dor. There's a main point gained: my lord is not married, I find. [*Aside.*

Mrs. Sul. But I wonder, friend, that in so many good services, you had not
a better provision made for you.

Arch. I don't know how, madam. I had a lieutenancy offered me three or
four times; but that is not bread, madam—I live much better as I
do.

Scrub. Madam, he sings rarely! I was thought to do pretty well here in the country till he came; but alack a day, I 'm nothing to my brother Martin!

Dor. Does he?—Pray, sir, will you oblige us with a song?

Arch. Are you for passion or humour?

Scrub. Oh le! he has the purest ballad about a trifle—

Mrs. Sul. A trifle! pray, sir, let's have it.

Arch. I 'm ashamed to offer you a trifle, madam; but since you command me—

[Sings to the tune of Sir Simon the King]

A trifling song you shall hear,
Begun with a trifle and ended:
All trifling people draw near,
And I shall be nobly attended.

Were it not for trifles, a few,
That lately have come into play;
The men would want something to do,
And the women want something to say.

What makes men trifle in dressing?
Because the ladies (they know)
Admire, by often possessing,
That eminent trifle, a beau.

When the lover his moments has trifled,
The trifle of trifles to gain:
No sooner the virgin is rifled,
But a trifle shall part 'em again.

What mortal man would be able
At White's half an hour to sit?
Or who could bear a tea-table,
Without talking of trifles for wit?

The court is from trifles secure,
Gold keys are no trifles, we see:
White rods are no trifles, I 'm sure,
Whatever their bearers may be.

But if you will go to the place,
Where trifles abundantly breed,
The levee will show you His Grace
Makes promises trifles indeed.

A coach with six footmen behind,
I count neither trifle nor sin:
But, ye gods! how oft do we find
A scandalous trifle within.

A flask of champagne, people think it
A trifle, or something as bad:
But if you 'll contrive how to drink it;
You 'll find it no trifle, egad!

A parson's a trifle at sea,
A widow's a trifle in sorrow:
A peace is a trifle to-day,
Who knows what may happen to-morrow!

A black coat a trifle may cloke,
Or to hide it, the red may endeavour:

But if once the army is broke,
We shall have more trifles than ever.

The stage is a trifle, they say,
The reason, pray carry along,
Because at every new play,
The house they with trifles so throng.

But with people's malice to trifle,
And to set us all on a foot:
The author of this is a trifle,
And his song is a trifle to boot.

Mrs. Sul. Very well, sir, we 're obliged to you.—Something for a pair of gloves. [*Offering him money.*

Arch. I humbly beg leave to be excused: my master, madam, pays me; nor dare I take money from any other hand, without injuring his honour, and disobeying his commands. [*Exit Archer and Scrub.*

Dor. This is surprising! Did you ever see so pretty a well-bred fellow?

Mrs. Sul. The devil take him for wearing that livery!

Dor. I fancy, sister, he may be some gentleman, a friend of my lord's, that his lordship has pitched upon for his courage, fidelity, and discretion, to bear him company in this dress, and who ten to one was his second too.

Mrs. Sul. It is so, it must be so, and it shall be so!—for I like him.

Dor. What! better than the Count?

Mrs. Sul. The Count happened to be the most agreeable man upon the place; and so I chose him to serve me in my design upon my husband. But I should like this fellow better in a design upon myself.

Dor. But now, sister, for an interview with this lord and this gentleman; how shall we bring that about?

Mrs. Sul. Patience! you country ladies give no quarter if once you be entered. Would you prevent their desires, and give the fellows no wishing-time? Look'ee, Dorinda, if my Lord Aimwell loves you or deserves you, he'll find a way to see you, and there we must leave it. My business comes now upon the tapis. Have you prepared your brother?

Dor. Yes, yes.

Mrs. Sul. And how did he relish it?

Dor. He said little, mumbled something to himself, promised to be guided by me—but here he comes.

Enter Squire Sullen.

Squire Sul. What singing was that I heard just now?

Mrs. Sul. The singing in your head, my dear; you complained of it all day.

Squire Sul. You're impertinent

Mrs. Sul. I was ever so, since I became one flesh with you.

Squire Sul. One flesh! rather two carcasses joined unnaturally together.

Mrs. Sul. Or rather a living soul coupled to a dead body.

Dor. So, this is fine encouragement for me!

Squire Sul. Yes, my wife shows you what you must do.

Mrs. Sul. And my husband shows you what you must suffer.

Squire Sul. 'Sdeath, why can't you be silent?

Mrs. Sul. 'Sdeath, why can't you talk?

Squire Sul. Do you talk to any purpose?

Mrs. Sul. Do you think to any purpose?

Squire Sul. Sister, hark'ee I—[*Whispers.*] I shan't be home till it be late. [*Exit.*

Mrs. Sul. What did he whisper to ye?

Dor. That he would go round the back way, come into the closet, and listen as I directed him. But let me beg you once more, dear sister, to drop this project; for as I told you before, instead of awaking him to kindness, you may provoke him to a rage; and then who knows how far his brutality may carry him?

Mrs. Sul. I 'm provided to receive him, I warrant you. But here comes the Count: vanish! [*Exit Dorinda.*

Enter Count Bellair.

Don't you wonder, Monsieur le Count, that I was not at church this afternoon?

Count Bel. I more wonder, madam, that you go dere at all, or how you dare to lift those eyes to heaven that are guilty of so much killing.

Mrs. Sul. If Heaven, sir, has given to my eyes with the power of killing the virtue of making a cure, I hope the one may atone for the other.

Count Bel. Oh, largely, madam, would your ladyship be as ready to apply the remedy as to give the wound. Consider, madam, I am doubly a prisoner; first to the arms of your general, then to your more conquering eyes. My first chains are easy—there a ransom may redeem me; but from your fetters I never shall get free.

Mrs. Sul. Alas, sir! why should you complain to me of your captivity, who am in chains myself? You know, sir, that I am bound, nay, must be tied up in that particular that might give you ease: I am like you, a prisoner of war—of war, indeed—I have given my parole of honour! would you break yours to gain your liberty?

Count Bel. Most certainly I would, were I a prisoner among the Turks; dis is your case, you 're a slave, madam, slave to the worst of Turks, a husband.

Mrs. Sul. There lies my foible, I confess; no fortifications, no courage, conduct, nor vigilancy, can pretend to defend a place where the cruelty of the governor forces the garrison to mutiny.

Count Bel. And where de besieger is resolved to die before de place.—Here will I fix [*Kneels*];—with tears, vows, and prayers assault your heart and never rise till you surrender; or if I must storm—Love and St. Michael!—And so I begin the attack.

Mrs. Sul. Stand off!—[*Aside.*] Sure he hears me not!—And I could almost wish—he did not!—The fellow makes love very prettily.—[*Aloud.*] But, sir, why should you put such a value upon my person, when you see it despised by one that knows it so much better?

Count Bel. He knows it not, though he possesses it; if he but knew the value of the jewel he is master of he would always wear it next his heart, and sleep with it in his arms.

Mrs. Sul. But since he throws me unregarded from him—

Count Bel. And one that knows your value well comes by and takes you up, is it not justice?

[*Goes to lay hold of her.*

Enter Squire Sullen with his sword drawn.

Squire Sul. Hold, villain, hold!

Mrs. Sul. [*Presenting a pistol.*] Do you hold!

Squire Sul. What! murder your husband, to defend your bully!

Mrs. Sul. Bully! for shame, Mr. Sullen, bullies wear long swords, the gentleman has none; he's a prisoner, you know. I was aware of your outrage, and prepared this to receive your violence; and, if occasion were, to preserve myself against the force of this other gentleman.

Count Bel. O madam, your eyes be bettre firearms than your pistol; they nevre miss.

Squire Sul. What! court my wife to my face!

Mrs. Sul. Pray, Mr. Sullen, put up; suspend your fury for a minute.

Squire Sul. To give you time to invent an excuse!

Mrs. Sul. I need none.

Squire Sul. No, for I heard every syllable of your discourse.

Count Bel. Ah! and begar, I tink the dialogue was vera pretty.

Mrs. Sul. Then I suppose, sir, you heard something of your own barbarity?

Squire Sul. Barbarity! 'oons, what does the woman call barbarity? Do I ever meddle with you?

Mrs. Sul. No.

Squire Sul. As for you, sir, I shall take another time.

Count Bel. Ah, begar, and so must I.

Squire Sul. Look'ee, madam, don't think that my anger proceeds from any concern I have for your honour, but for my own, and if you can contrive any way of being a whore without making me a cuckold, do it and welcome.

Mrs. Sul. Sir, I thank you kindly, you would allow me the sin but rob me of the pleasure. No, no, I 'm resolved never to venture upon the crime without the satisfaction of seeing you punished for't.

Squire Sul. Then will you grant me this, my dear? Let anybody else do you the favour but that Frenchman, for I mortally hate his whole generation.

[*Exit.*

Count Bel. Ah, sir, that be ungrateful, for begar, I love some of yours.— Madam—[*Approaching her.*

Mrs. Sul. No, sir.

Count Bel. No, sir! garzoon, madam, I am not your husband.

Mrs. Sul. 'Tis time to undeceive you, sir. I believed your addresses to me were no more than an amusement, and I hope you will think the same of my complaisance; and to convince you that you ought, you must know that I brought you hither only to make you instrumental in setting me right with my husband, for he was planted to listen by my appointment.

Count Bel. By your appointment?

Mrs. Sul. Certainly.

Count Bel. And so, madam, while I was telling twenty stories to part you from your husband, begar, I was bringing you together all the while?

Mrs. Sul. I ask your pardon, sir, but I hope this will give you a taste of the virtue of the English ladies.

Count Bel. Begar, madam, your virtue be vera great, but garzoon, your honeste be vera little.

Re-enter Dorinda.

Mrs. Sul. Nay, now, you 're angry, sir.

Count Bel. Angry!—*Fair Dorinda [Sings 'Fair Dorinda,' the opera tune, and addresses Dorinda.]* Madam, when your ladyship want a fool, send for me. *Fair Dorinda, Revenge, etc, [Exit singing.*

Mrs. Sul. There goes the true humour of his nation—resentment with good manners, and the height of anger in a song! Well, sister, you must be judge, for you have heard the trial.

Dor. And I bring in my brother guilty.

Mrs. Sul. But I must bear the punishment. Tis hard, sister.

Dor. I own it; but you must have patience.

Mrs. Sul. Patience! the cant of custom—Providence sends no evil without a remedy. Should I lie groaning under a yoke I can shake off, I were accessory to my ruin, and my patience were no better than self-murder.

Dor. But how can you shake off the yoke? your divisions don't come within the reach of the law for a divorce.

Mrs. Sul. Law! what law can search into the remote abyss of nature? what evidence can prove the unaccountable disaffections of wedlock? Can a jury sum up the endless aversions that are rooted in our souls, or can a bench give judgment upon antipathies?

Dor. They never pretended, sister; they never meddle, but in case of uncleanness.

74

Mrs. Sul. Uncleanness! O sister! casual violation is a transient injury, and may possibly be repaired, but can radical hatreds be ever reconciled? No, no, sister, nature is the first lawgiver, and when she has set tempers opposite, not all the golden links of wedlock nor iron manacles of law can keep 'em fast.

> *Wedlock we own ordain'd by Heaven's decree,*
> *But such as Heaven ordain'd it first to be;—*
> *Concurring tempers in the man and wife*
> *As mutual helps to draw the load of life.*

> *View all the works of Providence above,*
> *The stars with harmony and concord move;*
> *View all the works of Providence below,*
> *The fire, the water, earth and air, we know,*
> *All in one plant agree to make it grow.*

> *Must man, the chiefest work of art divine,*
> *Be doom'd in endless discord to repine?*
> *No, we should injure Heaven by that surmise,*
> *Omnipotence is just, were man but wise.*

[*Exeunt.*

ACT IV., SCENE I

The Gallery in Lady Bountiful's House, Mrs. Sullen discovered alone.

Mrs. Sul. Were I born an humble Turk, where women have no soul nor property, there I must sit contented. But in England, a country whose women are its glory, must women be abused? where women rule, must women be enslaved? Nay, cheated into slavery, mocked by a promise of comfortable society into a wilderness of solitude! I dare not keep the thought about me. Oh, here comes something to divert me.

Enter a Countrywoman.

Worn. I come, an't please your ladyship—you're my Lady Bountiful, an't ye?

Mrs. Sul. Well, good woman, go on.

Worn. I have come seventeen long mail to have a cure for my husband's sore leg.

Mrs. Sul. Your husband! what, woman, cure your husband!

Worn. Ay, poor man, for his sore leg won't let him stir from home.

Mrs. Sul. There, I confess, you have given me a reason. Well, good woman, I 'll tell you what you must do. You must lay your husband's leg upon a table, and with a chopping-knife you must lay it open as broad as you can, then you must takeout the bone, and beat the flesh soundly with a rolling-pin, then take salt, pepper, cloves, mace, and ginger, some sweet-herbs, and season it very well, then roll it up like brawn, and put it into the oven for two hours.

Worn. Heavens reward your ladyship!—I have two little babies too that are piteous bad with the graips, an't please ye.

Mrs. Sul. Put a little pepper and salt in their bellies, good woman.

Enter Lady Bountiful.

I beg your ladyship's pardon for taking your business out of your hands; I have been a-tampering here a little with one of your patients.

Lady Boun. Come, good woman, don't mind this mad creature; I am the person that you want, I suppose. What would you have, woman?

Mrs. Sul. She wants something for her husband's sore leg.

Lady Boun. What's the matter with his leg, goody?

Worn. It come first, as one might say, with a sort of dizziness in his foot, then he had a kind of laziness in his joints, and then his leg broke out, and then it swelled, and then it closed again, and then it broke out again, and then it festered, and then it grew better, and then it grew worse again.

Mrs. Sul. Ha! ha! ha!

Lady Boun. How can you be merry with the misfortunes of other people?

Mrs. Sul, Because my own make me sad, madam.

Lady Boun. The worst reason in the world, daughter; your own misfortunes should teach you to pity others.

Mrs. Sul. But the woman's misfortunes and mine are nothing alike; her husband is sick, and mine, alas! is in health.

Lady Boun. What! would you wish your husband sick?

Mrs. Sul. Not of a sore leg, of all things.

Lady Boun. Well, good woman, go to the pantry, get your bellyful of victuals, then I 'll give you a receipt of diet-drink for your husband.

But d'ye hear, goody, you must not let your husband move too much?

Worn. No, no, madam, the poor man's inclinable enough to lie still. [*Exit.*

Lady Boun. Well, daughter Sullen, though you laugh, I have done miracles about the country here with my receipts.

Mrs. Sul. Miracles indeed, if they have cured anybody; but I believe, madam, the patient's faith goes. farther toward the miracle than your prescription.

Lady Boun. Fancy helps in some cases; but there's your husband, who has as little fancy as anybody, I brought him from death's door.

Mrs. Sul. I suppose, madam, you made him drink plentifully of ass's milk.

Enter Dorinda, who runs to Mrs. Sullen.

Dor. News, dear sister! news! news!

Enter Archer, running.

Arch. Where, where is my Lady Bountiful?—Pray, which is the old lady of you three?

Lady Boun. I am.

Arch. O madam, the fame of your ladyship's charity, goodness, benevolence, skill and ability, have drawn me hither to implore your ladyship's help in behalf of my unfortunate master, who is this moment breathing his last.

Lady Boun. Your master! where is he?

Arch. At your gate, madam. Drawn by the appearance of your handsome house to view it nearer, and walking up the avenue within five paces of the courtyard, he was taken ill of a sudden with a sort of I know not what, but down he fell, and there he lies.

Lady Boun. Here, Scrub! Gipsy! all run, get my easy chair down stairs, put the gentleman in it, and bring him in quickly! quickly!

Arch. Heaven will reward your ladyship for this charitable act.

Lady Boun. Is your master used to these fits?

Arch. O yes, madam, frequently: I have known him have five or six of a night.

Lady Boun. What's his name?

Arch. Lord, madam, he 's a-dying! a minute's care or neglect may save or destroy his life.

Lady Boun. Ah, poor gentleman!—Come, friend, show me the way; I 'll see him brought in myself.

[Exit with Archer.

Dor. O sister, my heart flutters about strangely! I can hardly forbear running to his assistance.

Mrs. Sul. And I 'll lay my life he deserves your assistance more than he wants it. Did not I tell you that my lord would find a way to come at you? Love's his distemper, and you must be the physician; put on all your charms, summon all your fire into your eyes, plant the whole artillery of your looks against his breast, and down with him.

Dor. O sister! I 'm but a young gunner; I shall be afraid to shoot, for fear the piece should recoil, and hurt myself.

Mrs. Sul. Never fear, you shall see me shoot before you, if you will.

Dor. No, no, dear sister; you have missed your mark so unfortunately, that I shan't care for being instructed by you.

*Enter Aimwell in a chair carried by Archer and Scrubs and counterfeiting a swoon;
Lady Bountiful and Gipsy following.*

Lady Boun. Here, here, let's see the hartshorn drops.—Gipsy, a glass of fair water! His fit's very strong.—Bless me, how his hands are clinched!

Arch. For shame, ladies, what d' ye do? why don't you help us?—[*To Dorinda.*] Pray, madam, take his hand, and open it, if you can, whilst I hold his head.

[*Dorinda takes his hand.*

Dor. Poor gentleman!—Oh!—he has got my hand within his, and squeezes it unmercifully—
Lady Boun. 'Tis the violence of his convulsion, child.
Arch. Oh, madam, he's perfectly possessed in these cases—he'll bite if you don't have a care.
Dor. Oh, my hand! my hand!
Lady Boun. What's the matter with the foolish girl? I have got his hand open, you see, with a great deal of ease.
Arch. Ay, but, madam, your daughter's hand is somewhat warmer than your ladyship's, and the heat of it draws the force of the spirits that way.
Mrs. Sul. I find, friend, you're very learned in these sorts of fits.
Arch. Tis no wonder, madam, for I 'm often troubled with them myself; I find myself extremely ill at this minute. [*Looking hard at Mrs. Sullen.*
Mrs. Sul. I fancy I could find a way to cure you.

[*Aside.*

Lady Boun. His fit holds him very long.
Arch. Longer than usual, madam.—Pray, young lady, open his breast and give him air.
Lady Boun. Where did his illness take him first, pray?
Arch. To-day at church, madam.
Lady Boun. In what manner was he taken?

Arch. Very strangely, my lady. He was of a sudden touched with something in his eyes, which, at the first, he only felt, but could not tell whether 'twas pain or pleasure.

Lady Boun. Wind, nothing but wind!

Arch. By soft degrees it grew and mounted to his brain, there his fancy caught it; there formed it so beautiful, and dressed it up in such gay, pleasing colours, that his transported appetite seized the fair idea, and straight conveyed it to his heart That hospitable seat of life sent all its sanguine spirits forth to meet, and opened all its sluicy gates to take the stranger in.

Lady Boun. Your master should never go without a bottle to smell to.—Oh—he recovers! The lavender-water—some feathers to burn under his nose—Hungary water to rub his temples.—Oh, he comes to himself!—Hem a little, sir, hem.—Gipsy! bring the cordial-water.

[Aimwell seems to awake in amaze.

 Dor. How d' ye, sir?
 Aim. Where am I? *[Rising.*
 Sure I have pass'd the gulf of silent death,
 And now I land on the Elysian shore!—
 Behold the goddess of those happy plains,
 Fair Proserpine—let me adore thy bright divinity.

[Kneels to Dorinda, and kisses her hand.

Mrs. Sul. So, so, so! I knew where the fit would end!
Aim. Eurydice perhaps—
 How could thy Orpheus keep his word,
 And not look back upon thee?
 No treasure but thyself could sure have bribed him
 To look one minute off thee.

Lady Boun. Delirious, poor gentleman!

Arch. Very delirious, madam, very delirious.

Aim. Martin's voice, I think.

Arch. Yes, my Lord.—How does your lordship?

Lady Boun. Lord! did you mind that, girls?

[*A side to Mrs. Sullen and Dorinda.*

Aim. Where am I?

Arch. In very good hands, sir. You were taken just now with one of your old fits, under the trees, just by this good lady's house; her ladyship had you taken in, and has miraculously brought you to yourself, as you see.

Aim. I am so confounded with shame, madam, that I can now only beg pardon; and refer my acknowledgments for your ladyship's care till an opportunity offers of making some amends. I dare be no longer troublesome.—Martin! give two guineas to the servants. [*Going.*

Dor. Sir, you may catch cold by going so soon into the air; you don't look, sir, as if you were perfectly recovered.

[*Here Archer talks to Lady Bountiful in dumb show.*

Aim. That I shall never be, madam; my present illness is so rooted that I must expect to carry it to my grave.

Mrs. Sul. Don't despair, sir; I have known several in your distemper shake it off with a fortnight's physic.

Lady Boun. Come, sir, your servant has been telling me that you're apt to relapse if you go into the air: your good manners shan't get the better of ours—you shall sit down again, sir. Come, sir, we don't mind ceremonies in the country—here, sir, my service t'ye.—You shall taste my water; 'tis a cordial I can assure you, and of my own making—drink it off, sir.—[*Aimwell drinks.*] And how d'ye find yourself now, sir?

Aim. Somewhat better—though very faint still.

Lady Boun. Ay, ay, people are always faint after these fits.—Come, girls, you shall show the gentleman the house.—'Tis but an old family building, sir; but you had better walk about, and cool by degrees, than venture immediately into the air. You 'll find some tolerable pictures.—Dorinda, show the gentleman the way. I must go to the poor woman below. [*Exit.*

Dor. This way, sir.

Aim. Ladies, shall I beg leave for my servant to wait on you, for he understands pictures very well?

Mrs. Sul. Sir, we understand originals as well as he does pictures, so he may come along.

[*Exeunt all but Scrub, Aimwell leading Dorinda. Enter Foigard.*

Foi. Save you, Master Scrub!

Scrub. Sir, I won't be saved your way—I hate a priest, I abhor the French, and I defy the devil. Sir, I 'm a bold Briton, and will spill the last drop of my blood to keep out popery and slavery.

Foi. Master Scrub, you would put me down in politics, and so I would be speaking with Mrs. Shipsy.

Scrub. Good Mr. Priest, you can't speak with her; she's sick, sir, she's gone abroad, sir, she's—dead two months ago, sir.

Re-enter Gipsy.

Gip. How now, impudence! how dare you talk so saucily to the doctor?— Pray, sir, don't take it ill; for the common people of England are not so civil to strangers, as—

Scrub. You lie! you lie! 'tis the common people that are civilest to strangers.

Gip. Sirrah, I have a good mind to—get you out I say.

Scrub. I won't. .

Gip. You won't, sauce-box!—Pray, doctor, what, is the captain's name that came to your inn last night?

Scrub. [*Aside.*] The captain! ah, the devil, there she hampers me again; the captain has me on one side, and the priest on t' other: so between the gown and the sword, I have a fine time on't.—But, *Cedunt arma toga.* [*Going.*

Gip. What, sirrah, won't you march?

Scrub. No, my dear, I won't march—but I'll walk.—[*Aside.*] And I 'll make bold to listen a little too.

[*Goes behind the side-scene and listens.*

Gip. Indeed, doctor, the Count has been barbarously treated, that's the truth on't.

Foi. Ah, Mrs. Gipsy, upon my shoul, now, gra, his complainings would mollify the marrow in your bones, and move the bowels of your commiseration! He veeps, and he dances, and he fistles, and he swears, and he laughs, and he stamps, and he sings; in conclusion, joy, he's afflicted *à-la-Française*, and a stranger would not know whider to cry or to laugh with him.

Gip. What would you have me do, doctor?

Foi. Noting, joy, but only hide the Count in Mrs. Sullen's closet when it is dark.

Gip. Nothing! is that nothing? it would be both a sin and a shame, doctor.

Foi. Here is twenty louis-d'ors, joy, for your shame and I will give you an absolution for the shin.

Gip. Sut won't that money look like a bribe?

Foi. Dat is according as you shall tauk it. If you receive the money beforehand, 'twill be *logicè*, a bribe; but if you stay till afterwards, 'twill be only a gratification.

Gip. Well, doctor, I 'll take it *logicè* But what must I do with my conscience, sir?

Foi. Leave dat wid me, joy; I am your priest, gra; and your conscience is under my hands.

Gip. But should I put the Count into the closet—

Foi. Vel, is dere any shin for a man's being in a closhet? one may go to prayers in a closhet.

Gip. But if the lady should come into her chamber, and go to bed?

Foi. Vel, and is dere any shin in going to bed, joy?

Gip. Ay, but if the parties should meet, doctor?

Foi. Vel den—the parties must be responsible. Do you be gone after putting the Count into the closhet; and leave the shins wid themselves. I will come with the Count to instruct you in your chamber.

Gip. Well, doctor, your religion is so pure! Methinks I'm so easy after an absolution, and can sin afresh with so much security, that I 'm resolved to die a martyr to't Here's the key of the garden door, come in the back way when 'tis late, I 'll be ready to receive you; but don't so much as whisper, only take hold of my hand; I 'll lead you, and do you lead the Count, and follow me. [*Exeunt.*

Scrub. [*Coming forward.*] What witchcraft now have these two imps of the devil been a-hatching here? 'There 's twenty louis-d'ors'; I heard that, and saw the purse.—But I must give room to my betters.

[*Exit.*

Re-enter Aimwell, leading Dorinda, and making love in dumb show; Mrs. Sullen and Archer following.

Mrs. Sul. [*To Archer.*] Pray, sir, how d'ye like that piece?

Arch. Oh, 'tis Leda! You find, madam, how Jupiter comes disguised to make love—

Mrs. Sul. But what think you there of Alexander's battles?

Arch. We only want a Le Brun, madam, to draw greater battles, and a greater general of our own. The Danube, madam, would make a greater figure in a picture than the Granicus; and we have our Ramillies to match their Arbela.

Mrs. Sul. Pray, sir, what head is that in the corner there?

Arch. O madam, 'tis poor Ovid in his exile.

Mrs. Sul. What was he banished for?

Arch. His ambitious love, madam.—[*Bowing.*] His misfortune touches me.

Mrs. Sul. Was he successful in his amours?

Arch. There he has left us in, the dark. He was too much a gentleman to tell.

Mrs. Sul. If he were secret, I pity him.

Arch. And if he were successful, I envy him.

Mrs. Sul. How d 'ye like that Venus over the chimney?

Arch. Venus! I protest, madam, I took it for your picture; but now I look again, 'tis not handsome enough.

Mrs. Sul. Oh, what a charm is flattery! If you would see my picture, there it is over that cabinet. How d' ye like it?

Arch. I must admire anything, madam, that has the least resemblance of you. But, methinks, madam—[*He looks at the picture and Mrs. Sullen three or four times, by turns.*] Pray, madam, who drew it?

Mrs. Sul. A famous hand, sir.

[*Here Aimwell and Dorinda go off.*

Arch. A famous hand, madam!—Your eyes, indeed, are featured there; but where's the sparking moisture, shining fluid, in which they swim? The picture, indeed, has your dimples; but where's the swarm of killing Cupids that should ambush there? The lips too are figured out; but where's the carnation dew, the pouting ripeness that tempts the taste in the original?

Mrs. Sul. Had it been my lot to have matched with such a man! [*Aside.*

Arch. Your breasts too—presumptuous man! what, paint Heaven!— Apropos, madam, in the very next picture is Salmoneus, that was struck dead with lightning, for offering to imitate Jove's thunder; I hope you served the painter so, madam?

Mrs. Sul. Had my eyes the power of thunder, they should employ their lightning better.

Arch. There's the finest bed in that room, madam! I suppose 'tis your ladyship's bedchamber.

Mrs. Sul. And what then, sir?

Arch. I think the quilt is the richest that ever I saw. I can't at this distance, madam, distinguish the figures of the embroidery; will you give me leave, madam?

Mrs. Sul. [*Aside.*] The devil take his impudence!—Sure, if I gave him an opportunity, he durst not offer it?—I have a great mind to try.— [*Going: Returns.*] 'Sdeath, what am I doing?—And alone, too!—Sister! sister! [*Runs out.*

Arch. I 'll follow her close—

For where a Frenchman durst attempt to storm, A Briton sure may well the work perform. [*Going.*

Re-enter Scrub.

Scrub. Martin! brother Martin!

Arch. O brother Scrub, I beg your pardon, I was not a-going: here's a guinea my master ordered you.

Scrub. A guinea! hi! hi! hi! a guinea! eh—by this light it is a guinea! But I suppose you expect one-and-twenty shillings in change?

Arch. Not at all; I have another for Gipsy.

Scrub. A guinea for her! faggot and fire for the witch! Sir, give me that guinea, and I 'll discover a plot.

Arch. A plot!

Scrub. Ay, sir, a plot, and a horrid plot! First, it must be a plot, because there's a woman in't: secondly, it must be a plot, because there's a priest in't: thirdly, it must be a plot, because there 's French gold in't: and fourthly, it must be a plot, because I don't know what to make on't.

Arch. Nor anybody else, I 'm afraid, brother Scrub.

Scrub. Truly, I 'm afraid so too; for where there's a priest and a woman, there's always a mystery and a riddle. This I know, that here has been the doctor with a temptation in one hand and an absolution in the other, and Gipsy has sold herself to the devil; I saw the price paid down, my eyes shall take their oath on't.

Arch. And is all this bustle about Gipsy?

Scrub. That's not all; I could hear but a word here and there; but I remember they mentioned a Count, a closet, a back-door, and a key.

Arch. The Count!—Did you hear nothing of Mrs. Sullen?

Scrub. I did hear some word that sounded that way; but whether it was Sullen or Dorinda, I could not distinguish.

Arch. You have told this matter to nobody, brother?

Scrub. Told! no, sir, I thank you for that; I 'm resolved never to speak one word *pro* nor *con*, till we have a peace.

Arch. You're i' the right, brother Scrub. Here's a treaty afoot between the Count and the lady: the priest and the chambermaid are the plenipotentiaries. It shall go hard but I find a way to be included in the treaty.—Where 's the doctor now?

Scrub. He and Gipsy are this moment devouring my lady's marmalade in the closet.

Aim. [*From without.*] Martin! Martin!

Arch. I come, sir, I come.

Scrub. But you forget the other guinea, brother Martin.

Arch. Here, I give it with all my heart.

Scrub. And I take it with all my soul.—[*Exit Archer.*] Ecod, I 'll spoil your plotting, Mrs. Gipsy! and if you should set the captain upon me, these two guineas will buy me off. [*Exit.*

Re-enter Mrs. Sullen and Dorinda, meeting.

Mrs. Sul. Well, sister!

Dor. And well, sister!

Mrs. Sul. What's become of my lord?

Dor. What's become of his servant?

Mrs. Sul. Servant! he's a prettier fellow, and a finer gentleman by fifty degrees, than his master.

Dor. O' my conscience, I fancy you could beg that fellow at the gallows-foot!

Mrs. Sul. O' my conscience I could, provided I could put a friend of yours in his room.

Dor. You desired me, sister, to leave you, when you transgressed the bounds of honour.

Mrs. Sul. Thou dear censorious country girl! what dost mean? You can't think of the man without the bedfellow, I find.

Dor. I don't find anything unnatural in that thought: while the mind is conversant with flesh and blood, it must conform to the humours of the company.

Mrs. Sul. How a little love and good company improves a woman! Why, child, you begin to live—you never spoke before.

Dor. Because I was never spoke to.—My lord has told me that I have more wit and beauty than any of my sex; and truly I begin to think the man is sincere.

Mrs. Sul. You're in the right, Dorinda; pride is the life of a woman, and flattery is our daily bread; and she's a fool that won't believe a man there, as much as she that believes him in anything else. But I 'll lay you a guinea that I had finer things said to me than you had.

Dor. Done! What did your fellow say to ye?

Mrs. Sul. My fellow took the picture of Venus for mine.

Dor. But my lover took me for Venus herself.

Mrs. Sul. Common cant! Had my spark called me a Venus directly, I should have believed him a footman in good earnest.

Dor. But my lover was upon his knees to me.

Mrs. Sul. And mine was upon his tiptoes to me.

Dor. Mine vowed to die for me.

Mrs. Sul. Mine swore to die with me.

Dor. Mine spoke the softest moving things.

Mrs. Sul. Mine had his moving things too.

Dor. Mine kissed my hand ten thousand times,

Mrs. Sul. Mine has all that pleasure to come.

Dor. Mine offered marriage.

Mrs. Sul. O Lard! d' ye call that a moving thing?

Dor. The sharpest arrow in his quiver, my dear sister! Why, my ten thousand pounds may lie brooding here this seven years, and hatch nothing at last but some ill-natured clown like yours. Whereas if I marry my Lord Aimwell, there will be titled, place, and precedence, the Park, the play, and the drawing-room, splendour, equipage, noise, and flambeaux.—*Hey, my Lady Aimwell's servants there!—Lights, lights to the stairs!—My Lady Aimwell's coach put forward!—Stand by make room for her ladyship!*—Are not these things moving?—What! melancholy of a sudden?

Mrs. Sul. Happy, happy sister! your angel has been watchful for your happiness, whilst mine has slept regardless of his charge. Long smiling years of circling joys for you, but not one hour for me! [*Weeps.*

Dor. Come, my dear, we 'll talk of something else.

90

Mrs. Sul. O Dorinda! I own myself a woman, full of my sex, a gentle, generous soul, easy and yielding to soft desires; a spacious heart, where love and all his train might lodge. And must the fair apartment of my breast be made a stable for a brute to lie in?

Dor. Meaning your husband, I suppose?

Mrs. Sul. Husband! no; even husband is too soft a name for him.—But, come, I expect my brother here to-night or to-morrow; he was abroad when my father married me; perhaps he 'll find a way to make me easy.

Dor. Will you promise not to make yourself easy in the meantime with my lord's friend?

Mrs. Sul. You mistake me, sister. It happens with us as among the men, the greatest talkers are the greatest cowards? and there's a reason for it; those spirits evaporate in prattle, which might do more mischief if they took another course.—Though, to confess the truth, I do love that fellow;—and if I met him dressed as he should be, and I undressed as I should be—look 'ee, sister, I have no supernatural gifts—I can't swear I could resist the temptation; though I can safely promise to avoid it; and that's as much as the best of us can do.

[*Exeunt.*

ACT IV., SCENE II.

A Room in Bonifaces Inn. Enter Aimwell and Archer laughing.

Arch. And the awkward kindness of the good motherly old gentlewoman—

Aim. And the coming easiness of the young one—'Sdeath, 'tis pity to deceive her!

Arch. Nay, if you adhere to these principles, stop where you are.

Aim. I can't stop; for I love her to distraction.

Arch. 'Sdeath, if you love her a hair's-breadth beyond discretion, you must go no further. 9

Aim. Well, well, anything to deliver us from sauntering away our idle evenings at White's, Tom's, or Will's and be stinted to bare looking at our old acquaintance, the cards; because our impotent pockets can't afford us a guinea for the mercenary drabs.

Arch. Or be obliged to some purse-proud coxcomb for a scandalous bottle, where we must not pretend to our share of the discourse, because we can't pay our club o' th' reckoning.—Damn it, I had rather sponge upon Morris, and sup upon a dish of bones scored behind the door!

Aim. And there expose our want of sense by talking criticisms, as we should our want of money by railing at the government.

Arch. Or be obliged to sneak into the side-box, and between both houses steal two acts of a play, and because we han't money to see the other three, we come away discontented, and damn the whole five.

Aim. And ten thousand such rascally tricks—had we outlived our fortunes among our acquaintance.—But now—

Arch. Ay, now is the time to prevent all this:—strike while the iron is hot.—This priest is the luckiest part of our adventure; he shall marry you, and pimp for me.

Aim. But I should not like a woman that can be so fond of a Frenchman.

Arch. Alas, sir! Necessity has no law. The lady may be in distress; perhaps she has a confounded husband, and her revenge may carry her farther than her love. Egad, I have so good an opinion of her, and of myself, that I begin to fancy strange things: and we must say this for the honour of our women, and indeed of ourselves, that they do stick to their men as they do to their *Magna Charta,* If the plot lies as I suspect, I must put on the gentleman.—But here comes the doctor—I shall be ready. [*Exit.*

[*Enter Foigard.*]

Foi. Sauve you, noble friend.

Aim. O sir, your servant! Pray, doctor, may I crave your name?

Foi, Fat naam is upon me? My naam is Foigard, joy.

Aim. Foigard! a very good name for a clergyman. Pray, Doctor Foigard, were you ever in Ireland? Foi, Ireland! no, joy. Fat sort of plaace is dat saam Ireland? Dey say de people are catched dere when dey qre young.

Aim. And some of 'em when they are old:—as for example.—[*Takes Foigard by the shoulder.*] Sir, I arrest you as a traitor against the government; you're a subject of England, and this morning showed me a commission, by which you served as chaplain in the French army. This is death by our law, and your reverence must hang for it.

Foi. Upon my shoul, noble friend, dis is strange news you tell me! Fader Foigard a subject of England! de son of a burgomaster of Brussels, a subject of England! ubooboo—

Aim. The son of a bog-trotter in Ireland! Sir, your tongue will condemn you before any bench in the kingdom.

Foi. And is my tongue all your evidensh, joy?

Aim. That's enough.

Foi. No, no, joy, for I vill never spake English no more.

Aim. Sir, I have other evidence.—Here, Martin!

Re-enter Archer.

You know this fellow?

Arch. [*In a brogue.*] Saave you, my dear cussen, how does your health?

Foi. [*Aside.*] Ah! upon my shoul dere is my countryman, and his brogue will hang mine.—[*To Archer.*] Mynheer, *Ick wet neat watt hey xacht, Ick universton ewe neaty sacramant!*

Aim. Altering your language won't do, sir; this fellow knows your person, and will swear to your face.

Foi. Faash! fey, is dere a brogue upon my faash too?

Arch. Upon my soulvation dere ish, joy!—But cussen Mackshane, vil you not put a remembrance upon me?

Foi. Mackshane! by St. Paatrick, dat ish my naam shure enough! [*Aside.*

Aim. I fancy, Archer, you have it. [*Aside to Archer.*

Foi. The devil hang you, joy! by fat acquaintance are you my cussen?

Arch. Oh, de devil hang yourshelf, joy! you know we were little boys togeder upon de school, and your foster-moder's son was married upon my nurse's chister, joy, and so we are Irish cussens.

Foi. De devil taake de relation! vel, joy, and fat school was it?

Arch. I tinks it vas—aay—'twas Tipperary.

Foi. No, no, joy; it vas Kilkenny.

Aim. That 's enough for us—self-confession,——come, sir, we must deliver you into the hands of the next magistrate.

Arch. He sends you to jail, you 're tried next assizes, and away you go swing into purgatory.

94

Foi. And is it so wid you, cussen?

Arch. It vil be sho wid you, cussen, if you don't immediately confess the secret between you and Mrs. Gipsy. Look 'ee, sir, the gallows or the secret, take your choice.

Foi. The gallows! upon my shoul I hate that saam gallow, for it is a diseash dat is fatal to our family. Vel, den, dere is nothing, shentlemens, but Mrs. Shullen would spaak wid the Count in her chamber at midnight, and dere is no haarm, joy, for I am to conduct the Count to the plash, myshelf.

Arch. As I guessed.—Have you communicated the matter to the Count?

Foi. I have not sheen him since.

Arch. Right again! Why then, doctor—you shall conduct me to the lady instead of the Count.

Foi. Fat, my cussen to the lady! upon my shoul, gra, dat is too much upon the brogue.

Arch. Come, come, doctor; consider we have got a rope about your neck, and if you offer to squeak, we 'll stop your windpipe, most certainly: we shall have another job for you in a day or two, I hope.

Aim. Here 's company coming this way; let's into my chamber, and there concert our affairs farther.

Arch. Come, my dear cussen, come along. [*Exeunt.*

Enter Boniface, Hounslow, and Bagshot at one door, Gibbet at the opposite.

Gib. Well, gentlemen, 'tis a fine night for our enterprise.

Houn. Dark as hell.

Bag. And blows like the devil; our landlord here has showed us the window where we must break in, and tells us the plate stands in the wainscot cupboard in the parlour.

Bon. Ay, ay, Mr. Bagshot, as the saying is, knives and forks, and cups and cans, and tumblers and tankards. There's one tankard, as the saying is, that's near upon as big as me; it was a present to the squire from his godmother, and smells of nutmeg and toast like an East-India ship.

Houn. Then you say we must divide at the stairhead?

Bon. Yes, Mr Hounslow, as the saying is. At one end of that gallery lies my Lady Bountiful and her daughter, and at the other Mrs. Sullen. As for the squire—

Gib. He's safe enough, I have fairly entered him, and he's more than half seas over already. But such a parcel of scoundrels are got about him now, that, egad, I was ashamed to be seen in their company.

Bon. Tis now twelve, as the saying is—gentlemen, you must set out at one.

Gib. Hounslow, do you and Bagshot see our arms fixed, and I 'll come to you presently.

Houn.,Bag. We will. [*Exeunt.*

Gib. Well, my dear Bonny, you assure me that Scrub is a coward?

Bon. A chicken, as the saying is. You 'll have no creature to deal with but the ladies.

Gib. And I can assure you, friend, there's a great deal of address and good manners in robbing a lady; I am the most a gentleman that way that ever travelled the road.—But, my dear Bonny, this prize will be a galleon, a Vigo business.—I warrant you we shall bring off three of four thousand pounds.

Bon. In plate, jewels, and money, as the saying is, you may.

Gib. Why then, Tyburn, I defy thee! I'll get up to town, sell off my horse and arms, buy myself some pretty employment in the household, and be as snug and as honest as any courtier of 'em all.

Bon. And what think you then of my daughter Cherry for a wife?

Gib. Look 'ee, my'dear Bonny—Cherry *is the Goddess I adore*, as the song goes; but it is a maxim, that man and wife should never have it in their power to hang one another; for if they should, the Lord have mercy on 'em both! [*Exeunt.*

ACT V., SCENE I.

A Room in Bonifaces Inn, Knocking without, enter Boniface.

Bon. Coming! Coming!—A coach and six foaming horses at this time o'
    night I some great man, as the saying is, for he scorns to travel with
    other people.

Enter Sir Charles Freeman.

Sir Chas. What, fellow! a public house, and abed when other people sleep?

Bon. Sir, I an't abed, as the saying is.

Sir Chas. Is Mr. Sullen's family abed, think 'ee?

Bon. All but the squire himself, sir, as the saying is; he's in the house.

Sir Chas. What company has he?

Bon. Why, sir, there 's the constable, Mr. Gage the exciseman, the hunch-
    backed barber, and two or three other gentlemen.

Sir Chas. I find my sister's letters gave me the true picture of her spouse.
    [*Aside.*

Enter Squire Sullen, drunk.

Bon. Sir, here's the squire.

Squire Sul. The puppies left me asleep—Sir!

Sir Chas. Well, sir.

Squire Sul. Sir, I am an unfortunate man—I have three thousand pounds
    a year, and I can't get a man to drink a cup of ale with me.

Sir Chas. That's very hard.

Squire Sul. Ay, sir; and unless you have pity upon me, and smoke one pipe with me, I must e'en go home to my wife, and I had rather go to the devil by half.

Sir Chas. But I presume, sir, you won't see your wife to-night; she 'll be gone to bed. You don't use to lie with your wife in that pickle?

Squire Sul. What I not lie with my wife! why, sir, do you take me for an atheist or a rake?

Sir Chas. If you hate her, sir, I think you had better lie from her.

Squire Sul. I think so too, friend. But I'm a Justice of peace, and must do nothing against the law.

Sir Chas. Law! as I take it, Mr. Justice, nobody observes law for law's sake, only for the good of those for whom it was made.

Squire Sul. But, if the law orders me to send you to jail you must lie there, my friend.

Sir Chas. Not unless I commit a crime to deserve it

Squire Sul. A crime? 'oons, an't I martied?

Sir Chas. Nay, sir, if you call a marriage a crime, you must disown it for a law.

Squire Sul. Eh! I must be acquainted with you, sir.—But, sir, I should be very glad to know the truth of this matter.

Sir Chas. Truth, sir, is a profound sea, and few there be that dare wade deep enough to find out the bottom on't. Besides, sir, I 'm afraid the line of your understanding mayn't be long enough.

Squire Sul. Look'ee, sir, I have nothing to say to your sea of truth, but, if a good parcel of land can entitle a man to a little truth, I have as much as any He in the country.

Bon. I never heard your worship, as the saying is, talk so much before.

Squire Sul. Because I never met with a man that I liked before.

Bon. Pray, sir, as the saying is, let me ask you one question: are not man and wife one flesh?

Sir Chas. You and your wife, Mr. Guts, may be one flesh, because ye are nothing else; but rational creatures have minds that must be united.

Squire Sul. Minds!

Sir Chas. Ay, minds, sir; don't you think that the mind takes place of the body?

Squire Sul. In some people.

Sir Chas. Then the interest of the master must be consulted before that of his servant

Squire Sul. Sir, you shall dine with me to-morrow!—'Oons, I always thought that we were naturally one.

Sir Chas. Sir, I know that my two hands are naturally one, because they love one another, kiss one another, help one another in all the actions of life; but I could not say so much if they were always at cuffs.

Squire Sul. Then 'tis plain that we are two.

Sir Chas. Why don't you part with her, sir?

Squire Sul. Will you take her, sir?

Sir Chas. With all my heart.

Squire Sul. You shall have her to-morrow morning, and a venison-pasty into the bargain.

Sir Chas. You 'll let me have her fortune too?

Squire Sul. Fortune! why, sir, I have no quarrel at her fortune: I only hate the woman, sir, and none but the woman shall go.

Sir Chas. But her fortune, sir—

Squire Sul. Can you play at whisk, sir?

Sir Chas. No, truly, sir.

Squire Sul. Nor at all-fours?

Sir Chas. Neither.

Squire Sul. [*Aside.*] 'Oons! where was this man bred?—[*Aloud.*] Burn me, sir! I can't go home, 'tis but two a clock.

Sir Chas. For half an hour, sir, if you please; but you must consider 'tis late.

Squire Sul. Late! that's the reason I can't go to bed.—Come, sir! [*Exeunt.*

Enter Cherry, runs across the stage, and knocks at Aimwells chamber door. Enter Aimwell in his nightcap and gown.

Aim. What's the matter? you tremble, child; you're frighted.

Cher. No wonder, sir—But, in short, sir, this very minute a gang of rogues are gone to rob my Lady Bountiful's house.

Aim. How!

Cher. I dogged 'em to the very door, and left 'em breaking in.

Aim. Have you alarmed anybody else with the news?

Cher. No, no, sir, I wanted to have discovered the whole plot, and twenty other things, to your man Martin; but I have searched the whole house, and can't find him: where is he?

Aim. No matter, child; will you guide me immediately to the house?

Cher. With all my heart, sir; my Lady Bountiful is my godmother, and I love Mrs. Dorinda so well—

Aim. Dorinda! the name inspires me, the glory and the danger shall be all my own.—Come, my life, let me but get my sword. [*Exeunt.*

ACT V., SCENE II.

A Bedchamber in Lady Bountiful's House. Mrs. Sullen and Dorinda
discovered undressed; a table and lights.

Dor. 'Tis very late, sister, no news of your spouse yet?

Mrs. Sul. No, I 'm condemned to be alone till towards four, and then perhaps I may be executed with his company.

Dor. Well, my dear, I'll leave you to your rest; you 'll go directly to bed, I suppose?

Mrs. Sul. I don't know what to do.—Heigh-ho!

Dor. That's a desiring sigh, sister.

Mrs. Sul. This is a languishing hour, sister.

Dor. And might prove a critical minute if the pretty fellow were here.

Mrs. Sul. Here! what, in my bedchamber at two o'clock o' th' morning, I undressed, the family asleep, my hated husband abroad, and my lovely fellow at my feet!—O 'gad, sister!

Dor. Thoughts are free, sister, and them I allow you.—So, my dear, good night.

Mrs. Sul. A good rest to my dear Dorinda!—[*Exit Dorinda.*] Thoughts free! are they so? Why, then, suppose him here, dressed like a youthful, gay, and burning bridegroom, [Here Archer steals out of a closet behind. with tongue enchanting, eyes bewitching, knees imploring.]
—[*Turns a little on one side and sees Archer in the posture she describes.*]—Ah!—[*Shrieks, and runs to the other side of the stage.*] Have my thoughts raised a spirit?—What are you, sir, a man or a devil?

Arch. A man, a man, madam. [*Rising.*

Mrs. Sul. How shall I be sure of it?

Arch. Madam, I'll give you demonstration this minute.

[*Takes her hand.*

Mrs. Sul. What, sir! do you intend to be rude?

Arch. Yes, madam, if you please.

Mrs. Sul. In the name of wonder, whence came ye?

Arch. From the skies, madam—I'm a Jupiter in love, and you shall be my Alcmena.

Mrs. Sul. How came you in?

Arch. I flew in at the window, madam; your cousin Cupid lent me his wings, and your sister Venus opened the casement.

Mrs. Sul. I 'm struck dumb with wonder!

Arch. And I—with admiration!

[*Looks passionately at her.*

Mrs. Sul. What will become of me?

Arch. How beautiful she looks!—The teeming jolly Spring smiles in her blooming face, and, when she was conceived, her mother smelt to roses, looked on lilies—

Lilies unfold their white, their fragrant charms,
When the warm sun thus darts into their arms.

[*Runs to her.*

Mrs. Sul. Ah! [*Shrieks.*

Arch. 'Oons, madam, what d' ye mean? you 'll raise the house.

Mrs. Sul. Sir, I 'll wake the dead before I bear this!—What! approach me with the freedom of a keeper! I 'm glad on't, your impudence has cured me.

Arch. If this be impudence—[*Kneels.*] I leave to your partial self; no panting pilgrim, after a tedious, painful voyage, e'er bowed before his saint with more devotion.

Mrs. Sul. [*Aside.*] Now, now, I 'm ruined if he kneels!—[*Aloud.*] Rise, thou prostrate engineer, not all thy undermining skill shall reach my heart.—Rise, and know I am a woman without my sex; I can love to all the tenderness of wishes, sighs, and tears—but go no farther.—Still, to convince you-that I'm more than woman, I can speak my frailty, confess my weakness even for you, but—

Arch. For me! [*Going to lay hold on her.*

Mrs. Sul. Hold, sir! build not upon that; for my most mortal hatred follows if you disobey what I command you now.—Leave me this minute.—[*Aside.*] If he denies I 'm lost.

Arch. Then you 'll promise—

Mrs. Sul. Anything another time.

Arch. When shall I come?

Mrs. Sul. To-morrow—when you will.

Arch. Your lips must seal the promise.

Mrs. Sul. Psha!

Arch. They must! they must! [*Kisses her.*]—Raptures and paradise!—And why not now, my angel? the time, the place, silence, and secrecy, all conspire. And the now conscious stars have preordained this moment for my happiness. [*Takes her in his arms.*

Mrs. Sul. You will not! cannot, sure!

Arch. If the sun rides fast, and disappoints not mortals of to-morrow's dawn, this night shall crown my joys.

Mrs. Sul. My sex's pride assist me!

Arch. My sex's strength help me!

Mrs. Sul. You shall kill me first!

Arch. I 'll die with you. [*Carrying her off.*
Mrs. Sul. Thieves! thieves! murder!

Enter Scrub in his breeches, and one shoe.

Scrub. Thieves! thieves! murder! popery!
Arch. Ha! the very timorous stag will kill in rutting time. [*Draws, and offers to stab Scrub.*
Scrub. [*Kneeling.*] O pray, sir, spare all I have, and take my life!
Mrs. Sul. [*Holding Archer's hand.*] What does the fellow mean?
Scrub. O madam, down upon your knees, your marrow-bones!—he 's one of 'em.
Arch. Of whom?
Scrub. One of the rogues—I beg your pardon, one of the honest gentlemen that just now are broke into the house.
Arch. How!
Mrs. Sul. I hope you did not come to rob me?
Arch. Indeed I did, madam, but I would have taken nothing but what you might ha' spared; but your crying 'Thieves' has waked this dreaming fool, and so he takes 'em for granted.
Scrub. Granted! 'tis granted, sir; take all we have.
Mrs. Sul. The fellow looks as if he were broke out of Bedlam.
Scrub. 'Oons, madam, they 're broke into the house with fire and sword! I saw them, heard them; they 'll be here this minute.
Arch. What, thieves!
Scrub. Under favour, sir, I think so.
Mrs. Sul. What shall we do, sir?
Arch. Madam, I wish your ladyship a good night
Mrs. Sul. Will you leave me?
Arch. Leave you! Lord, madam, did not you command me to be gone just now, upon pain of your immortal hatred?
Mrs. Sul. Nay, but pray, sir—[*Takes hold of him.*

104

Arch. Ha! ha! ha! now comes my turn to be ravished.—You see now, madam, you must use men one way or other; but take this by the way; good madam, that none but a fool will give you the benefit of his courage, unless you'll take his love along with it.—How are they armed, friend?

Scrub. With sword and pistol, sir.

Arch. Hush!—I see a dark lantern coming through the gallery—Madam, be assured I will protect you, or lose my life.

Mrs. Sul. Your life! no, sir, they can rob me of nothing that I value half so much; therefore now, sir, let me entreat you to be gone.

Arch. No, madam, I'll consult my own safety for the sake of yours; I 'll work by stratagem. Have you courage enough to stand the appearance of 'em?

Mrs. Sul. Yes, yes, since I have 'scaped your hands, I can face anything.

Arch. Come hither, brother Scrub! don't you know me?

Scrub. Eh, my dear brother, let me kiss thee.

[*Kisses Archer.*

Arch. This way—here—
[Archer and Scrub hide behind the bed.

Enter Gibbet, with a dark lantern in one hand, and a pistol in the other.

Gib. Ay, ay, this is the chamber, and the lady alone.

Mrs. Sul. Who are you, sir? what would you have? d' ye come to rob me?

Gib. Rob you! alack a day, madam, I 'm only a younger brother, madam; and so, madam, if you make a noise, I 'll shoot you through the head; but don't be afraid, madam.—[*Laying his lantern and pistol upon the table.*] These rings, madam; don't be concerned, madam, I have a profound respect for you, madam; your keys, madam; don't be frighted, madam, I 'm the most of a gentleman.—[*Searching her pockets.*] This necklace, madam; I never was rude to any lady;—I have a veneration—for this necklace—

[*Here Archer having come round, and seized the pistol takes Gibbet by the collar, trips up his heels, and claps the pistol to his breast.*

Arch. Hold, profane villain, and take the reward of thy sacrilege!
Gib. Oh! pray, sir, don't kill me; I an't prepared.
Arch. How many is there of 'em, Scrub?
Scrub. Five-and-forty, sir.
Arch. Then I must kill the villain, to have him out of the way.
Gib. Hold, hold, sir, we are but three, upon my honour.
Arch. Scrub, will you undertake to secure him?
Scrub. Not I, sir; kill him, kill him!
Arch. Run to Gipsy's chamber, there you'll find the doctor; bring him hither presently.—[*Exit Scrub, running.*] Come, rogue, if you have a short prayer, say it.
Gib. Sir, I have no prayer at all; the government has provided a chaplain to say prayers for us on these occasions.
Mrs. Sul. Pray, sir, don't kill him: you fright me as much as him.
Arch. The dog shall die, madam, for being the occasion of my disappointment.—Sirrah, this moment is your last.
Gib. Sir, I 'll give you two hundred pounds to spare my life.
Arch. Have you no more, rascal?
Gib. Yes, sir, I can command four hundred, but I must reserve two of 'em to save my life at the sessions.

Re-enter Scrub and Foigard.

Arch. Here, doctor, I suppose Scrub and you between you may manage him. Lay hold of him, doctor.

[Foigard lays hold of Gibbet.

Gib. What! turned over to the priest already!—Look 'ee, doctor, you come before your time; I an't condemned yet, I thank ye.

Foi. Come, my dear joy; I vill secure your body and your shoul too; I vill make you a good catholic, and give you an absolution.

Gib. Absolution! can you procure me a pardon, doctor?

Foi. No, joy—

Gib. Then you and your absolution may to the devil!

Arch. Convey him into the cellar, there bind him:—take the pistol, and if he offers to resist, shoot him through the head—and come back to us with all the speed you can.

Scrub. Ay, ay, come, doctor, do you hold him fast, and I 'll guard him.

[Exit Foigard with Gibbet, Scrub following.

Mrs. Sul. But how came the doctor—

Arch. In short, madam—[*Shrieking without.*] 'Sdeath! the rogues are at work with the other ladies—I 'm vexed I parted with the pistol; but I must fly to their assistance.—Will you stay here, madam, or venture yourself with me?

Mrs. Sul. [*Taking him by the arm.*] Oh, with you, dear sir, with you. [*Exeunt.*

ACT V., SCENE III.

Another Bedchamber in the same. Enter Hounslow and Bagshot, with swords drawn, haling in Lady Bountiful and Dorinda.

Houn. Come, come, your jewels, mistress!
Bag. Your keys, your keys, old gentlewoman!

Enter Aimwell and Cherry.

Aim. Turn this way, villains! I durst engage an army in such a cause. [*He engages them both.*
Dor. O madam, had I but a sword to help the brave man!
Lady Boun. There's three or four hanging up in the hall; but they won't draw. I 'll go fetch one, however. [*Exit.*
Enter Archer and Mrs. Sullen.
Arch. Hold, hold, my lord! every man his bird, pray. [*They engage man to man; Hounslow and Bagshot are thrown and disarmed.*
Cher. [Aside.] What! the rogues taken! then they'll impeach my father: I must give him timely notice.

[*Runs out.*

Arch. Shall we kill the rogues?
Aim. No, no, we 'll bind them.
Arch. Ay, ay.—[*To Mrs. Sullen, who stands by him.*] Here, madam, lend me your garter.

Mrs. Sul. [*Aside.*] The devil's in this fellow! he fights, loves, and banters, all in a breath.—[*Aloud.*] Here's a cord that the rogues brought with 'em, I suppose.

Arch. Right, right, the rogue's destiny, a rope to hang himself.—Come, my lord—this is but a scandalous sort of an office [*Binding the Highwaymen together.*] if our adventures should end in this sort of hangman-work; but I hope there is something in prospect, that—

Enter Scrub.

Arch. Well, Scrub, have you secured your Tartar?

Scrub. Yes, sir, I left the priest and him disputing about religion.

Aim. And pray carry these gentlemen to reap the benefit of the controversy.

[*Delivers the prisoners to Scrubs who leads them out.*

Mrs. Sul. Pray, sister, how came my lord here?

Dor. And pray, how came the gentleman here?

Mrs. Sul. I 'll tell you the greatest piece of villainy—

[*They talk in dumb show.*

Aim. I fancy, Archer, you have been more successful in your adventures than the housebreakers.

Arch. No matter for my adventure, yours is the principal.—Press her this minute to marry you—now while she's hurried between the palpitation of her fear and the joy of her deliverance, now while the tide of her spirits is at high-flood—throw yourself at her feet, speak some romantic nonsense or other—address her, like Alexander in the height of his victory, confound her senses, bear down her reason, and away with her.—The priest is now in the cellar, and dare not refuse to do the work.

Re-enter Lady Bountiful.

Aim. But how shall I get off without being observed?

Arch. You a lover, and not find a way to get off!—Let me see—

Aim. You bleed, Archer.

Arch. 'Sdeath, I 'm glad on 't; this wound will do the business. I 'll amuse the old lady and Mrs. Sullen about dressing my wound, while you carry off Dorinda.

Lady Boun. Gentlemen, could we understand how you would be gratified for the services—

Arch. Come, come, my lady, this is no time for compliments; I 'm wounded, madam.

Lady Boun., Mrs. Sut. How! wounded!

Dor. I hope, sir, you have received no hurt?

Aim. None but what you may cure—

[Makes love in dumb show.

Lady Boun. Let me see your arm, sir—I must have some powder-sugar to stop the blood.—O me! an ugly gash; upon my word, sir, you must go into bed.

Arch. Ay, my lady, a bed would do very well.—*[To Mrs. Sullen.]* Madam, will you do me the favour to conduct me to a chamber.

Lady Boun. Do, do, daughter—while I get the lint and the probe and the plaster ready.

[Runs out one way, Aimwell carries off Dorinda another.

Arch. Come, madam, why don't you obey your mother's commands?

Mrs. Sul. How can you, after what is passed, have the confidence to ask me?

Arch. And if you go to that, how can you, after what is passed, have the confidence to deny me? Was not this blood shed in your defence, and my life exposed for your protection? Look 'ee, madam, I 'm none of your romantic fools, that fight giants and monsters for nothing; my valour is downright Swiss; I'm a soldier of fortune, and must be paid.'

Mrs. Sul. 'Tis ungenerous in you, sir, to upbraid me with your services!

Arch. 'Tis ungenerous in you, madam, not to reward 'em

Mrs. Sul. How! at the expense of my honour?

Arch. Honour! can honour consist with ingratitude? If you would deal like a woman of honour, do like a man of honour. D' ye think I would deny you in such a case?

Enter a Servant.

Serv. Madam, my lady ordered me to tell you, that your brother is below at the gate. [*Exit.*

Mrs. Sul. My brother! Heavens be praised!—Sir, he shall thank you for your services; he has it in his power.

Arch. Who is your brother, madam?

Mrs. Sul. Sir Charles Freeman.—You'll excuse me, sir; I must go and receive him. [*Exit.*

Arch. Sir Charles Freeman! 'sdeath and hell! my old acquaintance. Now unless Aimwell has made good use of his time, all our fair machine goes souse into the sea like the Eddystone. [*Exit.*

ACT V., SCENE IV.

The Gallery in the same house. Enter Aimwell and Dorinda.

Dor. Well, well, my lord, you have conquered; your late generous action
will, I hope, plead for my easy yielding; though I must own, your
lordship had a friend in the fort before.

Aim. The sweets of Hybla dwell upon her tongue!—Here, doctor—

Enter Foigard with a book.

Foi. Are you prepared boat?

Dor. I 'm ready. But first, my lord, one word.—I have a frightful example
of a hasty marriage in my own family; when I reflect upon't it shocks
me. Pray, my lord, consider a little—

Aim. Consider! do you doubt my honour or my love?

Dor. Neither: I do believe you equally just as brave: and were your whole sex
drawn out for me to choose, I should not cast a look upon the multitude
if you were absent. But, my lord, I'm a woman; colours, concealments
may hide a thousand faults in me, therefore know me better first; I
hardly dare affirm I know myself in anything except my love.

Aim. [Aside,] Such goodness who could injure! I find myself unequal to
the task of villain; she has gained my soul, and made it honest like
her own.—I cannot, cannot hurt her.—[*Aloud.*] Doctor, retire.—
[*Exit Foigard*] Madam, behold your lover and your proselyte, and
judge of my passion by my conversion!—I 'm all a lie, nor dare I
give a fiction to your arms; I 'm all counterfeit, except my passion.

Dor. Forbid it, Heaven! a counterfeit!

Aim. I am no lord, but a poor needy man, come with a mean, a scandalous design to prey upon your fortune; but the beauties of your mind and person have so won me from myself that, like a trusty servant, I prefer the interest of my mistress to my own.

Dor. Sure I have had the dream of some poor mariner, a sleepy image of a welcome port, and wake involved in storms!—Pray, sir, who are you?

Aim. Brother to the man whose title I usurped, but stranger to his honour or his fortune.

Dor. Matchless honesty!—Once I was proud, sir, of your wealth and title, but now am prouder that you want it: now I can show my love was justly levelled, and had no aim but love.—Doctor, come in.

Enter Foigard at one door, Gipsy at another-, who whispers Dorinda.

[*To Foigard.*] Your pardon, sir, we shan't want you now.—[*To Aimweil.*] Sir, you must excuse me—I 'll wait on you presently. [*Exit with Gipsy.*

Foi. Upon my shoul, now, dis is foolish. [*Exit.*

Aim. Gone! and bid the priest depart!—It has an ominous look.

Enter Archer.

Arch. Courage, Tom!—Shall I wish you joy?

Aim. No.

Arch. 'Oons, man, what ha' you been doing?

Aim. O Archer! my honesty, I fear, has ruined me.

Arch. How?

Aim. I have discovered myself.

Arch. Discovered! and without my consent? What! have I embarked my small remains in the same bottom with yours, and you dispose of all without my partnership?

Aim. O Archer! I own my fault.

Arch. After conviction—'tis then too late for pardon.—You may remember, Mr. Aimwell, that you proposed this folly: as you begun, so end it. Henceforth I 'll hunt my fortune single—so farewell!

Aim. Stay, my dear Archer, but a minute.

Arch. Stay! what, to be despised, exposed, and laughed at! No, I would sooner change conditions with the worst of the rogues we just now bound, than bear one scornful smile from the proud knight that once I treated as my equal.

Aim. What knight?

Arch. Sir Charles Freeman, brother to the lady that I had almost—but no matter for that, 'tis a cursed night's work, and so I leave you to make the best on't. [*Going.*

Aim. Freeman!—One word, Archer. Still I have hopes; methought she received my confession with pleasure.

Arch. 'Sdeath, who doubts it?

Aim. She consented after to the match; and still I dare believe she will be just.

Arch. To herself, I warrant her, as you should have been.

Aim. By all my hopes she comes, and smiling comes!

Re-enter Dorinda, mighty gay.

Dor. Come, my dear lord—I fly with impatience to your arms—the minutes of my absence were a tedious year. Where's this priest?

Re-enter Foigard.

Arch. 'Oons, a brave girl!

Dor. I suppose, my lord, this gentleman is privy to our affairs?

Arch. Yes, yes, madam, I 'm to be your father.

Dor. Come, priest, do your office.

Arch. Make haste, make haste, couple 'em any way.—[*Takes Aimwells hand.*]
   Come, madam, I 'm to give you—
Dor. My mind's altered; I won't.
Arch. Eh!
Aim. I 'm confounded!
Foi. Upon my shoul, and sho is myshelf.
Arch. What 's the matter now, madam?
Dor. Look'ee, sir, one generous action deserves another.—This gentleman's
   honour obliged him to hide nothing from me; my justice engages
   me to conceal nothing from him. In short, sir, you are the person
   that you thought you counterfeited; you are the true Lord Viscount
   Aimwell, and I wish your Lordship joy.—Now, priest, you may be
   gone; if my Lord is pleased now with the match, let his Lordship
   marry me in the face of the world.
Aim., Arch. What does she mean?
Dor. Here's a witness for my truth.

   Enter Sir Charles Freeman and Mrs Sullen.

Sir Chas. My dear Lord Aimwell, I wish you joy.
Aim. Of what?
Sir Chas. Of your honour and estate. Your brother died the day before I
   left London; and all your friends have writ after you to Brussels;—
   among the rest I did myself the honour.
Arch. Hark 'ee, sir knight, don't you banter now?
Sir Chas. 'Tis truth, upon my honour.
Aim. Thanks to the pregnant stars that formed this accident!
Arch. Thanks to the womb of time that brought it forth!—away with it!
Aim. Thanks to my guardian angel that led me to the prize! [*Taking
   Dorindas hand*].
Arch. And double thanks to the noble Sir Charles Freeman.—My Lord, I
   wish you joy.—My Lady, I wish you joy.—Egad, Sir Freeman, you're

the honestest fellow living!—'Sdeath, I'm grown strange airy upon this matter!—My Lord, how d'ye?—A word, my Lord; don't you remember something of a previous agreement, that entitles me to the moiety of this lady's fortune, which I think will amount to five thousand pounds?

Aim. Not a penny, Archer; you would ha' cut my throat just now, because I would not deceive this lady.

Arch. Ay, and I 'll cut your throat again, if you should deceive her now.

Aim. That's what I expected; and to end the dispute, the lady's fortune is ten thousand pounds, we'll divide stakes: take the ten thousand pounds or the lady.

Dor. How! is your lordship so indifferent?

Arch. No, no, no, madam! his Lordship knows very well that I 'll take the money; I leave you to his Lordship, and so we 're both provided for.

Enter Count Bellair.

Count Bel. *Mesdames et Messieurs,* I am your servant trice humble! I hear you be rob here.

Aim. The ladies have been in some danger, sir.

Count Bel. And, begar, our inn be rob too!

Aim. Our inn! by whom?

Count Bel. By the landlord, begar!—Garzoon, he has rob himself, and run away!

Arch. Robbed himself!

Count Bel. Ay, begar, and me too of a hundre pound.

Arch. A hundred pounds?

Count Bel. Yes, that I owed him.

Aim. Our money's gone, Frank.

Arch. Rot the money! my wench is gone.—[*To Count Bellair.*] *Savez-vous quelquechase de Mademoiselle Cherry?*

Enter a Countryman with a strong-box and a letter.

Coun. Is there one Martin here?

Arch. Ay, ay—who wants him?

Coun. I have a box here, and letter for him.

Arch. [*Taking the box.*] Ha! ha! ha! what's here? Legerdemain!—By this light, my lord, our money again!—But this unfolds the riddle.—[*Opening the letter.*] Hum, hum, hum!—Oh, 'tis for the public good, and must be communicated to the company.

[*Reads.*

Mr. Martin,

My father being afraid of an impeachment by the rogues that are taken to-night, is gone off; but if you can procure him a pardon, he'll make great discoveries that may be useful to the country. Could I have met you instead of your master to-night, I would have delivered myself into your hands, with a sum that much exceeds that in your strong-box, which I have sent you, with an assurance to my dear Martin that I shall ever be his most faithful friend till death.

CHERRY BONIFACE.

There's a billet-doux for you! As for the father, I think he ought to be encouraged; and for the daughter—pray, my Lord, persuade your bride to take her into her service instead of Gipsy.

Aim. I can assure you, madam, your deliverance was owing to her discovery.

Dor. Your command, my Lord, will do without the obligation. I 'll take care of her.

117

Sir Chas. This good company meets opportunely in favour of a design I have in behalf of my unfortunate sister. I intend to part her from her husband—gentlemen, will you assist me?

Arch. Assist you! 'sdeath, who would not?

Count Bel. Assist! garzoon, we all assist!

Enter Squire Sullen.

Squire Sul. What 's all this? They tell me, spouse, that you had like to have been robbed.

Mrs. Sul. Truly, spouse, I was pretty near it, had not these two gentlemen interposed.

Squire Sul. How came these gentlemen here?

Mrs. Sul. That's his way of returning thanks, you must know.

Count Bel. Garzoon, the question be apropos for all dat.

Sir Chas. You promised last night, sir, that you would deliver your lady to me this morning.

Squire Sul. Humph!

Arch. Humph! what do you mean by humph? Sir, you shall deliver her— in short, sir, we have saved you and your family; and if you are not civil, we 'll unbind the rogues, join with 'em, and set fire to your house. What does the man mean? not part with his wife!

Count Bel. Ay, garzoon, de man no understan common justice.

Mrs. Sul. Hold, gentlemen, all things here must move by consent, compulsion would spoil us; let my dear and I talk the matter over, and you shall judge it between us.

Squire Sul. Let me know first who are to be our judges. Pray, sir, who are you?

Sir Chas. I am Sir Charles Freeman, come to take away your wife.

Squire Sul. And you, good sir?

Aim. Thomas, Viscount Aimwell, come to take away your sister.

Squire Sul. And you, pray, sir?

118

Arch. Francis Archer, esquire, come—

Squire Sul. To take away my mother, I hope. Gentlemen, you 're heartily welcome; I never met with three more obliging people since I was born!—And now, my dear, if you please, you shall have the first word.

Arch. And the last, for five pounds!

Mrs. Sul. Spouse!

Squire Sul. Rib!

Mrs. Sul. How long have we been married?

Squire Sul. By the almanac, fourteen months; but by my account, fourteen years.

Mrs. Sul. 'Tis thereabout by my reckoning.

Count Bel. Garzoon, their account will agree.

Mrs. Sul. Pray, spouse, what did you marry for?

Squire Sul. To get an heir to my estate.

Sir Chas. And have you succeeded?

Squire Sul. No.

Arch. The condition fails of his side.—Pray, madam, what did you marry for?

Mrs. Sul. To support the weakness of my sex by the strength of his, and to enjoy the pleasures of an agreeable society.

Sir Chas. Are your expectations answered?

Mrs. Sul. No.

Count Bel. A clear case! a clear case!

Sir Chas. What are the bars to your mutual contentment?

Mrs. Sul. In the first place, I can't drink ale with him.

Squire Sul. Nor can I drink tea with her.

Mrs. Sul. I can't hunt with you.

Squire Sul. Nor can I dance with you.

Mrs. Sul. I hate cocking and racing.

Squire Sul. And I abhor ombre and piquet.

Mrs. Sul. Your silence is intolerable.

Squire Sul. Your prating is worse.

Mrs. Sul. Have we not been a perpetual offence to each other? a gnawing
vulture at the heart?

Squire Sul. A frightful goblin to the sight?

Mrs. Sul. A porcupine to the feeling?

Squire Sul. Perpetual wormwood to the taste?

Mrs. Sul. Is there on earth a thing we could agree in?

Squire Sul. Yes—to part.

Mrs. Sul. With all my heart

Squire Sul. Your hand.

Mrs. Sul. Here.

Squire Sul. These hands joined us, these shall part us.—Away!

Mrs. Sul. North

Squire Sul. South.

Mrs. Sul. East.

Squire Sul. West—far as the poles asunder.

Count Bel. Begar, the ceremony be vera pretty!

Sir Chas. Now, Mr. Sullen, there wants only my sister's fortune to make
us easy.

Squire Sul. Sir Charles, you love your sister, and I love her fortune; every
one to his fancy.

Arch. Then you won't refund;

Squire Sul. Not a stiver.

Arch. Then I find, madam, you must e'en go to your prison again.

Count Bel. What is the portion?

Sir Chas. Ten thousand pounds, sir.

Count Bel. Garzoon, I 'll pay it, and she shall go home wid me.

Arch. Ha! ha! ha! French all over.—Do you know, sir, what ten thousand
pounds English is?

Count Bel. No, begar, not justement.

Arch. Why, sir, 'tis a hundred thousand livres.

Count Bel. A hundre tousand livres! Ah! garzoon, me canno' do't, your beauties and their fortunes are both too much for me.

Arch. Then I will.—This night's adventure has proved strangely lucky to us all—for Captain Gibbet in his walk had made bold, Mr. Sullen, with your study and escritoir, and had taken out all the writings of your estate, all the articles of marriage with this lady, bills, bonds, leases, receipts to an infinite value: I took 'em from him, and I deliver 'em to Sir Charles.

[Gives Sir Charles Freeman a parcel of papers and parchments.

Squire Sul. How, my writings!—my head aches consumedly.—Well, gentlemen, you shall have her fortune, but I can't talk. If you have a mind, Sir Charles, to be merry, and celebrate my sister's wedding and my divorce, you may command my house—but my head aches consumedly.—Scrub, bring me a dram.

Arch. [*To Mrs. Sullen.*] Madam, there's a country dance to the trifle that I sung to-day; your hand, and we'll lead it up.

Here a Dance.

Twould be hard to guess which of these parties is the better pleased, the couple joined, or the couple parted; the one rejoicing in hopes of an untasted happiness, and the other in their deliverance from an experienced misery. Both happy in their several states we find, Those parted by consent, and those conjoined. Consent, if mutual, saves the lawyer's fee. Consent is law enough to set you free.

[Exeunt omnes.

EPILOGUE

Designed to be spoken in 'The Beaux-Stratagem'.

If to our play your judgment can't be kind, Let its expiring author pity find: Survey his mournful case with melting eyes, Nor let the bard be damn'd before he dies. Forbear, you fair, on his last scene to frown, But his true exit with a plaudit crown; Then shall the dying poet cease to fear The dreadful knell, while your applause he hear. At Leuctra so the conquering Theban died, Claim'd his friends' praises, but their tears denied: Pleased in the pangs of death he greatly thought Conquest with loss of life but cheaply bought The difference this, the Greek was one would fight As brave, though not so gay, as Serjeant Kite; Ye sons of Will's, what's that to those who write? To Thebes alone the Grecian owed his bays, You may the bard above the hero raise, Since yours is greater than Athenian praise.

Lightning Source UK Ltd.
Milton Keynes UK
UKHW022317080223
416651UK00001B/81